SEVENS

WEEK 4:
MELTDOWN

Scott Wallens

PUFFIN BOOKS

Meltdown

Puffin Books
Published by the Penguin Group
Penguin Putnam Books for Young Readers,
345 Hudson Street, New York, New York 10014, U.S.A.
Penguin Books Ltd, 80 Strand, London WC2R 0RL, England
Penguin Books Australia Ltd, Ringwood, Victoria, Australia
Penguin Books Canada Ltd, 10 Alcorn Avenue, Toronto, Ontario, Canada M4V 3B2
Penguin Books (N.Z.) Ltd, 182-190 Wairau Road, Auckland 10, New Zealand

Penguin Books Ltd, Registered Offices: Harmondsworth, Middlesex, England

Published by Puffin Books,
a division of Penguin Putnam Books for Young Readers, 2002

3 5 7 9 10 8 6 4 2

Front cover photography copyright © 2001 Steve Belkowitz/FPG
Back cover photography copyright (top to bottom) Stewart Cohen/Stone,
David Roth/Stone, David Rinella, Steve Belkowitz/FPG, Karan Kapoor/Stone,
David Lees/FPG, Mary-Arthur Johnson/FPG

Produced by 17th Street Productions,
an Alloy, Inc. company
151 West 26th Street
New York, NY 10001

17th Street Productions and associated logos
are trademarks and/or registered trademarks of Alloy, Inc.

ISBN 0-14-230101-9

Printed in the United States of America

CHAPTER ONE

"Okay, Jane, concentrate, concentrate, concentrate," Jane Scott mumbles to herself as she chews on her thumbnail. She stares down at the open history book in front of her, the words blurring and sharpening, blurring and sharpening. The sentences run together, and she can't seem to make sense of any of them.

Japanese-American populations of the Pacific Northwest . . . the staggering numbers in Washington State alone . . . ripped . . . forced . . . kept as prisoners . . . what Hitler had done and the free world condemned . . .

Jane's eyes flit to the open notebook next to the textbook. The blank page that should be full of notes by now. The sight of its emptiness, its clean blue lines, makes her stomach clench. She's supposed to be writing a paper on the Japanese internment camps in the United States during World War II.

If she's not doing that, then she should be doing her AP calculus problems.

Or her French homework.

1

Or her college applications.

Or her articles for the student Web site.

Or practicing her sax.

But she's not doing any of those things. What she is doing is sitting alert in her desk chair, chewing on her thumbnail, and listening for the mailman. It's ten-thirty on Saturday morning. Jane is at her father's house. Her mother's mail always arrives before her father's, so as soon as the mailman arrives here, she'll know her mother's mail is there. And if her mother's mail is there, that means her SAT scores could be there. And if her mother gets to her SAT scores before she does . . .

Jane glances at the clock: 10:31. God, she hates being at her dad's these days. Hates not being able to watch over the mailbox at her mother's house—her official residence, according to the Educational Testing Service. It's the worst form of self-torture she could ever devise.

"I can do this," Jane says to herself, slapping her hands down on the desk and pushing herself up in her seat. She takes a deep breath and lets it out slowly, hoping it will soothe her nerves.

But the deep breath does nothing. Jane feels like there's a constant current of electricity moving through her body, causing her dark skin to pull taut, her scalp to tingle.

There's nothing you can do about it, she tells herself. *If the scores come today, they come today. At least it will all be over.*

Jane stares at the pink Princess phone that matches the

pink room that her father put together for her in his house after her parents divorced five years ago. She waits for it to ring. Knows what her mother will sound like on the other end. Excited. Imploring.

"Jane? Your scores are here. Can I open them? I'll read them to you. . . ."

Jane knows she'll hear the envelope ripping before she even has a chance to answer.

The pink phone mocks her with every second of silence. Jane hates that phone. She's never liked pink. Not even when she was a little girl. But her father had thought Pepto-painted walls and coordinating accessories would make her feel at home at his place and she's never had the heart to tell him otherwise.

There's a knock. Jane jumps, then glares at the door.

"Jane, sweetie, it's your dad. Can I come in?" he whispers. Whispers. In his own house, when there's no one home but the two of them. It's always been his way, to treat his house like a library. It made being a child in his presence decidedly unfun.

"It's open, Dad," Jane calls out, louder than necessary.

Instinctively she picks up her pen and bends over the book again, copying out a random line from the textbook into her notes. *The internment camps were nothing more than barren expanses of land. . . .*

"There's my girl," Jane's father says, his tone proud as he eyes her studious posture and the stack of books on the floor

3

next to her chair. He walks up behind her and plants a kiss on top of her mop of dark kinky hair. "Hard at work, I see."

As always, Jane thinks. "Yep," she says brightly.

"Well, if I can tear you away for a moment, I have exciting news," he tells her. He sits on the edge of her bed, his large frame causing the springs to squeal in protest.

"I'm actually pretty busy," Jane says, already feeling her shoulders starting to curl in toward her chest.

"You can take a break to hear this, Janie," he says. The words are light, but the tone is no-nonsense. Jane sets her pen down and turns to look at her father.

"Sorry," Jane says, her expression blank. "What's up?"

Her father is always making ceremonious announcements about events that have no bearing on her life. Like that his firm is going to be buying up and remodeling a new strip mall five towns away and the development means "big money" for him and his partners. And the only thing Jane ever gets out of her father's acquisition of "big money" is more cash in her college fund. For a college she's never going to attend.

"You and I are going to Boston next weekend!" her father says with a grin.

Jane's curled shoulders rise up to almost touch her earlobes.

"We're what?" she says. She has never gone away with her father in her lifetime. Not one family vacation, weekend away, day at the beach ever included her father. It was always just her and her mom while Dad stayed home to work.

This cannot be a pleasure trip. There must be an ulterior motive. "What about Mom?" she says.

"What about your mother?" The grin never falters.

"I'll be at Mom's next weekend," Jane reminds him.

"Oh, she won't mind," her father says with an overexaggerated scoff that shows he knows his ex-wife *will* mind. A lot. "This is an important trip. We'll be visiting Harvard . . . MIT . . . BC. . . . Your mother will have to agree that exploring your opportunities is much more important than some arbitrary custody rule. Besides, you're old enough to make your own decisions about your time."

A laugh bubbles up in Jane's throat, but she swallows it back. She wonders if her dad's ever noticed that she hasn't made a decision about her own life since she was five and she'd decided to get a blue bike instead of green. Jane's forehead wrinkles for a moment as she tries to remember the last big decision in her life that her parents didn't make for her. She comes up blank.

Harvard . . . MIT . . . BC . . .

Her mother isn't just going to mind. Her mother is going to throw a fit of unprecedented proportions. And not because of the custody rule violation, but because of the list of schools. Not one conservatory among them. There's no way Jane's mother will let Jane's father get away with taking her to visit schools that have no music program to speak of.

Jane's eyes fall on the corner of her bed—the corner she always stashes her sax under when she comes to stay for the weekend. As a rule she doesn't like to leave it out when she's at her father's. He knows it's there somewhere, but as long as it's not in his face, he won't remember to tell her how impractical it is.

"When are you going to tell Mom about this?" Jane asks, knowing the trick answer to the straightforward question.

"Well, Janie, I thought you would ask her yourself," her father says.

You never even asked me *if* I *wanted to go!* Jane wants to shout. But even if he had asked her, she knows she would have said yes. It's not like she would have ever told the truth. Told him that this trip is pointless because she's never going to get into the schools he listed. She'll never even get into the lesser schools in Boston—the ones he hasn't even deigned to recognize. She isn't going to be going anywhere.

Jane hears the putter of the mail truck as it pulls to a stop in front of the house. She hears the creak of the mailbox door as it swings down, the plastic pop as it's closed. She forces herself to swallow. It seems like any second the phone will ring, and she dreads it with every fiber of her being.

"Sure, Dad," she tells him, realizing she has to say something. "I'll ask her."

Because right now all she wants is for him to get out of her room.

• • •

"One last question, Reed. What's it feel like to be *the man?*" The young, cute, curly-haired reporter from the

6

Winetka Tribune smirks as she holds out her mini tape recorder toward Reed Frasier's chin.

"Uhhh . . ." Reed scratches at the back of his head and laughs self-consciously. "Am I the man? I didn't exactly realize that."

She clicks off the recorder and slips it into her bag in one fluid motion. "Modest, too. I like it," she says. She makes a few notes on a steno pad and squints up at him, shielding her eyes from the sun with her hand. "Thanks, Reed. I'll speak to you after your next win." She grins as she smoothly turns and walks away, her sneakers crunching through the long-fallen leaves that bury the sidelines.

"Dude, did you *see* that?" Reed says, turning to his friend Jeremy Mandile, who's waiting for him next to the bench. "That girl so wants me."

"So much for modesty," Jeremy says, shaking his head. He slaps Reed's shoulder pad as they make their way across the field toward the school, trailing after the rest of the team, the parents, and half the student body.

Reed takes a deep breath of the crisp, cold November air and holds it in his lungs for a moment. He studies the school in front of him, wanting to remember this scene just the way it is. Blue sky, nearly leafless trees, hordes of people dressed in blue and gold to support the team. Reed passed for over a hundred yards and two touchdowns and has just had his first big interview for the sports section. The whole experience has filled him with a sense of pride that makes him feel about three feet taller. Reed wonders if his older brother, T. J., felt like this every time he was interviewed over the last three years. Every time he won big. No wonder the guy has such a monster ego.

Granted, T. J. is a lovable guy, but even *he'd* admit that he has an ego.

"Guys!" Karyn Aufiero calls out. Reed can't see her, but he'd know her voice anywhere just from the little thrill it sends down his spine. He and Jeremy stop and slowly turn to see Karyn jogging toward them, pleated miniskirt flying. Reed's heart flips at the sight of her and instead of making it stop midway as he usually does, he lets it execute the whole somersault. Why not? After all, it's his day, not T. J.'s. For once he's going to ignore the fact that Karyn is his brother's girlfriend.

"Hey, Aufiero," Reed says lightly. "What's the rush?"

But the moment she's close enough for him to see her face, his insides seem to hollow out. Something's wrong. Something big.

"What is it?" Reed asks, taking a step closer to Karyn.

She looks from Jeremy, to Reed, and back to Jeremy again. The smile on Jeremy's face fades as well.

"Don't freak or anything," Karyn says, holding out one hand as she searches blindly in her backpack with the other. She keeps her eyes trained on Jeremy's face. "I just heard from Gemma who heard from Maureen who heard from Cori Lerner that Danny Chaiken was in an accident last

8

night." She pauses and takes a deep breath. "They said his little sisters were in the car . . . and so was Emily."

Reed's stomach drops and he looks at Jeremy. Emily is Jeremy's little sister and probably the person Jeremy loves more than anyone in the world. She's friends with Danny Chaiken's little sisters, which would account for her being in the car.

"Here," Karyn says, finally pulling her cell phone out of her backpack. She hands it to Jeremy. "I'm sure everything's fine."

Visibly shaking, Jeremy drops his football helmet and quickly dials his number. All Reed and Karyn can do is wait. Reed doesn't breathe as he waits for Jeremy to speak.

"Emily? Emily! Oh, thank . . . are you okay?"

Jeremy looks up at his friends and nods. The relief in his eyes is contagious.

"I knew she'd be fine," Karyn whispers to Reed, crossing her arms over the front of her cheerleading sweater. "They would have called him if she hadn't been . . . right?"

"I'm sure," Reed says, though he isn't. Jeremy's parents have done a lot of things recently that no one expected. Like shutting out their son after he told them he was gay. Like refusing to understand that he was still the same person. Like just standing back while Jeremy moved in with Reed because he didn't feel comfortable in his own home.

"Good . . . I'm glad," Jeremy says, holding his free hand over his free ear. "No, you don't have to put Dad on the . . . Hi, Dad."

Reed's chest tightens as he sees Jeremy tense up. There's a pause as he listens. His eyes squeeze shut.

"Well, that's because I just found out! If you guys had called me—" He's shouting now. "No . . . no! What do you mean, if I had been there? What are you . . . you know what, Dad? Dad . . . ? *Dad!* I'm hanging up now."

Jeremy pulls the phone away from his ear and Reed can still hear Mr. Mandile as his friend fumbles with the keypad. Karyn finally reaches over and hits the little red button. With a beep, the voice is cut dead.

"Emily's fine," Jeremy says, reaching down to snatch his helmet up off the ground. "My dad tried to make it seem like it was somehow my fault that the whole thing happened, but other than that, it was a great conversation," he adds sarcastically. He starts to double-time it toward the gym entrance and Reed and Karyn scurry to catch up.

Reed has no idea what to say, but he's not surprised when Karyn slips her arm through Jeremy's, even though it's caked with dirt and sweat, and looks up at him, her face creased with concern.

"At least she's okay. That's what's important," Karyn says in a soothing tone. "Your dad is probably just stressed over the accident."

"I know," Jeremy says, tipping his head forward. "I'm sure he's on edge."

"Exactly. Just give him a chance to cool down," Karyn says with a smile.

She looks over at Reed and her eyes widen, prompting him to say something.

"Uh . . . why don't we all go somewhere and chill?" he suggests as they push through the back doors into the gym. "The mall or the diner or something?"

"Sounds good to me," Jeremy says.

Karyn graces Reed with an approving smile and the guys head off to the locker room to shower and change. Reed shakes his sweaty hair back off his face as he feels the sense of pride he felt a few moments ago return. But this time it's not because he's a football god. It's because of Karyn. Not only because she liked his suggestion, but because of who she is. She knew exactly how to handle the Emily situation, exactly what to say to Jeremy after he spoke to his dad.

She's so amazing, he thinks as he glances back at her, waiting for them in the middle of the gym. She's crouching down to retie her sneaker, and her ponytail is flipped forward to cover her face. Reed smiles, touched by the sheer intimacy of catching her off guard. Then all at once his face hardens and he pushes through the door to the locker room.

Why does she have to be so amazing?

• • •

This isn't happening to me. This isn't happening, Danny Chaiken tells himself on Saturday afternoon. *I did not just wake up in a hospital bed. I did not get into an accident and almost kill my sisters.*

He takes a deep breath and looks down at his hands through tear-filled eyes. The problem is, Danny Chaiken is not deluded. So he knows it's all true. He knows what he's done and why he's here. He can't make himself not believe it.

I'm such a jerk. No . . . not a jerk. That's not strong enough for what I did. There are no words strong enough for what I did.

Danny presses his eyes closed as thoughts and images cloud his brain, each fighting for control. He sees himself pretending to take his medication in front of his parents and the school nurses. Sees their trusting faces watching him as he deceives them.

But I had to. I had *to. I was losing it. Losing myself* . . . He sees himself spacing out in the middle of class when he was on his meds, dozing off at his desk, becoming a zombie incapable of writing, thinking . . . feeling. *I had to. . . .*

Then a picture flashes through his mind that shoves all the other thoughts out with one, sickening jolt. His sister, Abby, knocked out in the passenger seat of the car. Blood spilling down her face.

Because of me, Danny thinks, crossing his arms over his chest and pinching at his sides as he sinks farther down in his bed. *Because I hadn't been taking my medication. It's all my fault. Because I can't control myself. Why do I have to be like this? It's not fair. It's not fair. It's not—*

"Uh . . . Danny?" An uncertain voice breaks through the deafening cacophony of thoughts.

Danny opens his eyes and looks at the doorway to his

12

antiseptic, blue-and-white hospital room. His vision is blurred from the force with which he'd been squeezing his eyes shut and as they clear, he sees Jeremy Mandile standing there in his varsity jacket, his hands in the back pockets of his jeans, his hair wet from a recent shower.

Danny narrows his eyes, confused. He knows he has a concussion. Is it making him hallucinate?

"Hey, man," the hallucination says. "Can I come in?"

It's not until Danny nods in response and Jeremy steps into the room that he believes Jeremy is actually there. Why would Jeremy Mandile, a guy he's barely spoken to in the last seven years, be visiting him in the hospital? Then in a rush he realizes what's going on. Jeremy found out that Danny crashed his car while he was driving Emily Mandile home from dance class. Jeremy is here to kick his ass.

Danny pushes himself up straight in bed, causing a mind-bending pain to shoot through his skull. Adrenaline courses through his veins and momentarily clears his brain so that he can assess the situation—which is hopeless. It's not like he can defend himself from this bed. But Jeremy wouldn't really kick his butt when he's laid up in the hospital, would he? Danny knows Jeremy has a rep for being a nice guy, but under the circumstances, who knows what a person might do? And so Danny does the only thing he can think of to defend himself—he starts to babble.

"I'm so sorry, man, but Emily is okay. She's fine. She wasn't even scratched, I swear. And I never would have—"

"It's okay," Jeremy says, crossing to the foot of Danny's bed. "I know. I talked to Emily earlier."

"Oh," Danny says. He takes a deep breath, looks at Jeremy skeptically. "Then why are you . . . here?"

Jeremy laughs. "I know you probably think I'm insane, but I just wanted to see how you were doing. I've heard about all the stuff that's been going on . . . you know . . . with Boyle and being suspended and now this. . . . I just thought . . . you know." Jeremy shrugs and looks at Danny, obviously hoping he'll understand. When Danny just blinks back at him, baffled, Jeremy reddens a bit and raises his shoulders. "I guess I just thought you could use a friendly face. Considering everything that's happened to me lately, I know how much it matters to have some . . . support, I guess."

Danny is completely floored. For once in his life, he has no words. Here's this guy who barely knows him, who's been going through his own huge load of drama lately, and he's taking time out to be there for the guy who almost killed his sister? What is this, *Touched by an Angel*?

"Uh . . . thanks, man," Danny says, running his hand through his sandy hair. For the first time since he woke up in this place, he feels his nerves start to calm a bit. "I mean it. Thanks."

"Hey, it's no problem," Jeremy says. He perches on the edge of the rickety chair next to the bed. "So . . . how are your sisters?"

Danny's heart twists in his chest. "They're okay," he says.

"Abby got a few stitches in her forehead, but she'll be fine. And Jenny wasn't hurt."

"Good," Jeremy says, quickly glancing around the room. "So, what's the deal? Are they keeping you here?"

The instant Jeremy says the words, all the hairs on Danny's arms stand on end and he realizes his pulse is still racing. He wants to get out of this place so bad, he can *taste* it.

"I don't know," he says, glancing at the door. "My parents are talking to the doctors. I have a concussion, so they kept me overnight, but hopefully I'll be going home soon."

Danny hears his parents' voices approaching the door and Jeremy stands up the moment they walk in. Danny's mother's face goes white when she sees his visitor.

"Jeremy? What are you doing here? Is Emily all right?" she asks.

"Oh yeah. . . yes, Emily's fine," Jeremy says. "I was just here to say hi to Danny."

"Oh, thank God," Danny's mother says, pushing her hands into her short blond hair. "When I saw you, I just thought—"

"Everything's fine," Jeremy says with a reassuring smile. "We were just wondering when they're going to spring Danny."

"We just filled out the paperwork," Danny's father says, placing his hands on his wife's shoulders. "Actually, Jeremy, if you don't mind, we need to talk to our son."

Danny's heart drops at the serious tone in his father's voice and he looks at Jeremy. Still, what's the guy going to

15

do? Refuse to leave so that Danny's parents can't lace into him for what he's done?

You deserve everything you're about to get, Danny thinks. *Remember that.*

"Okay," Jeremy says, glancing at Danny. "I guess I'll see you in school."

"Yeah, man. Thanks," Danny says.

His parents pull both the chairs in the room up to the side of Danny's bed and sit down. They look completely exhausted. Danny knows they've probably been up all night, trying to figure out how to deal with him. He feels a white-hot bolt of resentment. He's always hated the implication that he is someone who needs to be handled.

But you are, a little voice in Danny's head reminds him. *Look what you've done.*

In a split second the resentment is replaced by guilt. Guilt for what he's put his parents through. Guilt for what he's put his sisters through. Guilt over the fact that if he hadn't been so selfish as to go off his meds, he could have prevented it all from happening.

"Daniel," his father says, folding his hands in his lap. "Your mother and I . . . well . . . I hate to say it, son, but I have to be honest. We're at the end of our rope here."

Danny looks at his mother's weary eyes, at the deep lines in his father's face. He wonders if they'd look as old as they do if they'd never had him to deal with.

"We don't know what to do anymore, Danny," his

mother says. "What's going on with you? And please don't tell me I won't understand. I'm sick of hearing that from you whenever something goes wrong," she adds, an edge of anger in her voice.

Danny can tell she's trying to keep it at bay—trying not to make a scene in the middle of the hospital. But if he tells them the truth, he knows she won't be able to contain it anymore. The thought of coming clean, of telling them how he's betrayed their trust, makes his stomach coil up into a ball of fear.

You have to tell them. You have to start being honest with them or this guilt is going to take over completely, Danny thinks, looking down at the plain white hospital blanket. *And you have to go back on your medication. It's time to start over.*

But it's your body, a defiant little voice in his head pipes up. *You should be able to decide what goes in it and what doesn't. You should be allowed to feel.*

Danny takes a deep breath and tries to shut that voice down. He can't pay attention to that logic anymore. He can't. Not if the result is car crashes, hospitals, stitches in his sister's forehead.

You'll just have to deal with the fog, Danny tells himself, his hands balling into fists as he tries not to resent the very thought. *You'll have to.*

"We're waiting, son," his father says.

"You guys are going to hate me," Danny says, trying to screw up his courage. Trying to bypass the paralyzing fear.

17

He holds his breath, then blurts out the truth before he can stop himself. "I went off my meds." There's a sharp intake of breath from his mother. Danny once again tucks his hands under his arms and pinches at the flesh on his sides. "About a week ago. I stopped taking them."

There's a long, drawn-out silence. And just when Danny's starting to believe his parents are never going to speak to him again, his mother freaks out.

"How *could* you?" she shouts. "How could you do that without telling us? Without telling your doctor?" She's standing now, her watery eyes bulging from her face. "How could you put yourself in danger like that? Not just yourself, but everyone around you! You could all have been killed! You could have killed someone else!"

"Mom, I—"

"I don't want to hear it, Danny!" his mother yells as his dad gets up and tries to calm her back into her chair. "I don't want to hear your explanations! Your *sisters* were in that car! Your little sisters, Danny! Not to mention Emily Mandile!"

At that moment, Danny is overwhelmed by tears. A choking sob escapes his throat and he tips his head forward and cries. He hates the fact that he's made his mother look at him that way. But at the same time he hates that she doesn't understand what it's like to be him—to not know who you are off your drugs—to be in a position where your family is afraid of you if you're not medicated into numbness.

But he also cries because he knows he was wrong. He's

never been so scared as when he saw Abby bleeding in the seat next to him. Not even on that day when he was little. The day that changed his life forever. Seeing his sister hurt and knowing he was responsible was the single worst moment of his life. And it didn't have to happen. It wouldn't have happened if Danny had been doing what he was supposed to be doing and taking his meds.

"I'm sorry," he says through his sobs as his parents watch him from the edge of the bed. "I'm so sorry."

• • •

Jane sits at her father's desk in the living room, bent over her French homework, quickly conjugating the list of verbs. Her pen flies so quickly over the page, anyone who saw her would think that French is her native language. Jane is in the zone. And when she's in the zone, it's like her brain and writing hand are working independently.

Suddenly the phone rings, and Jane's eyes dart up. What time is it? As the phone rings again, she searches the room for a clock like a person who has just woken up from a nap in an unfamiliar room. Finally she manages to focus on the VCR. It's eight o'clock in the evening.

Wait a minute . . . eight o'clock? Where has the day gone?

As Jane reels from the fact that the last time she looked up from her work, it was light out, she realizes that there's no reason to panic. It can't be her mother on the other end of the line. If her scores had come today, her mother would have called hours ago.

"Jane? It's for you," her father says, walking into the room. He's wearing an apron around his waist as he holds out the cordless phone. For the first time she notices the smell in the air. The strong scent of her father's vegetarian chili. How did that not penetrate her senses before?

"Do you know who it is?" Jane whispers, her heart giving a thump as she looks at the little holes in the mouthpiece of the phone. Maybe it *is* her mom. Maybe she was just out all day. Who else would be calling her here? Who even has her father's number?

"It's Sumit," her father says with a pleased light in his eyes. Jane's father likes Sumit Sachdeva. Not so much because he's incredibly smart, but because he's incredibly smart yet still not as smart as Jane.

Resisting the urge to roll her eyes at her dad, Jane takes the phone. Sumit is one of her best friends from school. A friend and a competitor. But then, all of Jane's friends are also academic competitors. They take all the same AP credits, are on the Academic Decathlon team together, and are constantly jockeying for class rank positions.

"Hey, Sumit," she says. "What's up?"

"Not much. Regina and I were just wondering if you felt like a movie," Sumit says brightly. "We're going to the nine-fifteen of *American Renegade* at the eightplex."

"*American Renegade?*" Jane repeats, her nose scrunching. She looks up at her father, who's still hovering, and he sticks out his tongue to show his distaste. Jane giggles. Still, bad action flick or not, it would be nice just to get away from the books for a moment. "Hold on a sec," she says into the receiver.

Covering the mouthpiece, Jane raises her eyebrows at her dad. "Can I go?" she asks. "It's at nine-fifteen." Jane can already taste the buttery popcorn and feel the soothing effects of sitting in a dark room staring at a pointless movie for two hours. Suddenly she's salivating, more for the freedom from work than from the thought of junk food.

"I don't know, Janie," her father says as he eyes her books. "Are you done with your work?"

Jane stares at him. "No . . . ," she says slowly. "But there's always tomorrow."

"It's your call," he says with a shrug and a disappointed sigh. "But you did say you had a lot to get done. And isn't there an Academic Decathlon meet coming up? Why aren't you and Sumit preparing for that?"

Jane slumps in her chair. Technically, he isn't saying no, but Jane has known her father long enough to hear what he isn't saying. He doesn't approve. And therefore, she's going nowhere.

She brings the phone back to her ear, stares down at the desk, the visions of freedom and popcorn vanishing before her eyes. "Sorry, Sumit," she says. "I can't. Maybe some other time."

There's a pause, and Jane knows Sumit is trying to decide from her tone whether it's okay to press her.

"Okay, some other time," Sumit says. "See you on Monday."

"Tell Regina I said hi," Jane says before clicking off the phone.

Her father walks over to her and takes the cordless, squeezing her shoulder with his free hand—his way of telling her she made the right decision. Then, without a word, he disappears into the kitchen.

Why am I doing this? Jane thinks, looking down at her French work. *Why am I wasting my time studying when it's not going to matter?*

She's been asking herself this question a lot lately. After all, the SAT scores that she's been waiting for have already been sent to all the schools she intended to apply to—all the Ivies and conservatories her parents handpicked. When she'd signed up for the test, she'd innocently checked the box asking the testing service to release the scores, never thinking there would be any reason to wait—any reason to keep the schools from seeing how she'd performed.

But now . . . now that those schools have her scores, she's sure they've already made a decision about her. And if that's the case, why is she still working? Why is she turning down movies to do work when there's no point?

Jane suddenly realizes she's wringing her hands in her lap and holding her breath. She lets it out slowly and releases her grip on herself. She has to keep working. If she doesn't keep working, it will be like admitting defeat—accepting reality. And if Jane has to face reality head-on, she's not sure she'll survive it. And she *knows* her parents won't.

Everything is going to be fine, she tells herself. As long as the scores haven't come. As long as there's no definitive proof of her failure, she can still calm herself down with the lie. *Everything's going to be fine. Somehow. Somehow it will.*

Taking a deep breath, Jane picks up her pen and returns to her work.

CHAPTER TWO

Meena Miller wakes up with a start on Sunday morning, the back of her neck drenched with sweat. Her long, dark hair sticks to her cheeks and forehead as she scrunches her stinging eyes shut against the harsh glare of sunlight streaming through her windows.

Was that a knock? her brain demands foggily, vaguely feeling as though some sort of noise caused her to wake up. Something not from the nightmare that is now quickly fading away into the ether. Not that she would have wanted to hang on to the slipping images anyway. From her ragged breathing, her pounding pulse, and the fact that she's clutching the corner of her pillow in her fist, she's actually quite glad that she can't remember a thing.

Another knock. More awake now, Meena whips her head to the left and glances at her alarm clock. It's ten A.M. Meena's heart drops. How is that possible? Her internal clock always, *always* wakes her before the sun comes up. That is, if she sleeps at all. What's wrong with her?

"Meena? It's Steven." She pulls her legs up toward her chin, hugging them to her. "Your mother asked me to come get you for breakfast."

The moment he says it, the smells hit Meena. It's as if her senses are waking up one at a time, and scent has just kicked in. The sweet aroma of pancakes mixed with the even sweeter scent of fried bacon conspire to make Meena smile, even as her stomach turns.

Her mother is making her favorite breakfast. Something Meena used to look forward to with an innocent excitement every week. And she's actually hungry. For the first time since she can remember, she feels like she could really eat a whole meal. But there's no way she's going down there. Not with Steven standing between her and the stairs. Not if he may be sitting across from her at the table, watching her every move.

"I'll be downstairs," Steven says.

It's just information, but to Meena it sounds like a threat. Everything Steven Clayton says sounds like a threat. And why shouldn't it? The man raped her. He hurt her in a way Meena had never thought she could be hurt. And now, because his house has burned to the ground and because her clueless parents happen to be friends with him, he's living in her house.

As he moves away from the door, Meena launches herself out of bed and rushes over to her dresser, pulling out clothes at random. She dresses quickly, pulling on jeans, a T-shirt, a sweater, and mismatched socks. Her hands are shaking with

25

fear, as well as the hunger that the smells in the house have awakened.

It's not fair, Meena thinks, blinking back tears. Hasn't Steven Clayton taken enough from her already? Now he has to take away her favorite weekly ritual, her time with her family, anything and everything that makes her feel safe and seminormal?

Meena pulls her jacket on over her bulky sweater and opens her bedroom door. The scents are even stronger and she has to close her eyes to keep from crying. She can't even sleep late in her own house without suffering the consequences. Without having something else snatched away from her. She wants so much to go down there and have breakfast with her family, but she can't stand the thought of sitting at the table with Steven. Can't even fathom it. But she doesn't know how she's going to explain her absence from the table to her parents.

So instead, she's just going to go. Get out of here. It's what she's been doing a lot lately.

Taking a deep breath and holding it, Meena rushes down the stairs, stepping lightly, and lets herself out the back door into the frigid November air. She's so jittery that she almost drops her keys as she heads for her car, but she manages to get it started and is out of the driveway before anyone can possibly notice she's gone.

The steering wheel is like a block of ice as she steers through the foggy town of Winetka Falls, watching the clouds her breath makes float in front of her. She shouldn't be out here in the cold by herself. She should be at the table with her mom and dad, talking about school and friends and sports. But Meena can't remember the last time that actually happened. She knows that it was well before Steven Clayton and his family moved in. Well before he became a constant in Meena's life.

Well before he ripped away her last shred of innocence.

A few minutes later Meena pushes her way through the glass-and-chrome door at the diner and drops down into her usual booth. It's not the crowd she's used to. Late night regulars like the truckers and the people from the A.A. meetings held nightly across the street have given way to laughing families and freshly showered couples poring over crisp newspapers. Meena feels like a vagrant with her dirty hair and her wrinkled clothes. She hunkers down in the booth and is almost relieved when Norma—good old Norma the waitress who seems to spend every waking hour working—makes her way over to her table.

"Coffee?" Norma asks, taking out her pad and pencil with no sense of irony. A stunning feat, considering coffee is the one and only thing Meena has ever ordered from the woman. Well, she's in for a shocker this morning.

"I'd like pancakes, bacon, a large orange juice, *and* a coffee," Meena says, staring straight ahead at the rip in the bench on the other side of the booth.

"Wow," Norma says. She snaps her gum once and writes it down. "I guess wonders *will* never cease."

Meena doesn't even try to smile. She likes Norma, but at this moment she doesn't have it in her. All she feels is grim determination to get every last bit of the food she just ordered into her stomach. Steven may have stolen her family and run her out of her house, but she isn't going to let him take anything else away from her. Not anymore.

• • •

"Okay, Danny, this is what we're going to do."

Danny watches his father blankly as he sits down across the dining-room table from him along with Danny's mother. Slumped down so far in his chair he's almost coming off the edge, Danny can't help thinking that this feels like some kind of summit meeting. Peace talks or something.

Or a parole hearing. He should be wearing an orange jumpsuit with an ID number stamped across the breast. He lifts his hands to put them up on the table, but his arms feel heavy and he lets them drop back down in his lap.

Danny does not want to do this, but he knows he has to. He doesn't want to be here, but then, he doesn't want to be in his room or in the living room or basically anywhere in the world. He wishes he could be someone else, but he's wished for that so many times in his life to no avail, he knows it's pointless.

He's always going to be who he is. Danny Chaiken. The insane, bipolar loser who can't even control himself. It's so pathetic. *He* is so pathetic.

No . . . pointless, that's what I am, Danny thinks. *I'm pointless.*

"Danny, sit up," his father says sternly, his brown eyes all business. "This is important."

Danny sighs and uses every ounce of energy in his body to push himself up about four inches. He sees his father and his mother exchange a look of resigned understanding and knows what they're thinking. *He must be in a low.* It's so depressing, knowing that his parents pity him.

But it's true, Danny is on a depressive swing. And it's bad. Really, really bad.

It's your own fault, idiot, he tells himself. *You're the one who went off your medication. Obviously your swings are going to be more severe. Hasn't Lansky told you that five thousand times? How stupid* are *you?*

His parents had called Dr. Lansky the day before and his psychiatrist had told them that he should go right back on his old dosage until he "normalized" again—then they will discuss a new medication. Something that might not make Danny as foggy and numb as he gets on the pills he's taking now.

Danny bites at the inside of his cheek, wondering if it's even possible. If he's ever going to "normalize." Yesterday he was a ball of nervous energy. Today he almost couldn't lift himself out of bed.

"We're going to call your principal today—at home— and tell him that you went off your meds," Danny's father says finally, resting his forearms on the table. He sounds like he's talking to a five-year-old.

"At home?" Danny says. As if Principal Maloney doesn't

hate him enough already after what he did last week. He's going to *love* having his Sunday afternoon interrupted by a call from the Chaikens.

"His number's on the PTA list," his mother explains. "We just want to get this resolved as soon as possible."

"We hope that if he knows there's a reason for your outburst the other day, he'll let you remain in school," Danny's father continues, running a hand over his balding head.

Who cares? Danny thinks, picking at a loose thread coming out of one of his belt loops. *I don't care if I never go back to school. It's not like I'm ever going to do anything with my life. Not if I'm like this.*

He glances across the table and realizes his parents are staring at him, waiting for him to say something. Right. He's supposed to be happy about this plan. Happy about going back to school.

"Okay . . . good," Danny says.

His father glances at Danny's mother again, asking a question with his eyes, and Danny's mother just looks back as if to say, "You do it." Danny fills with a sickening dread.

"What?" he asks. "What is it?"

His father slowly turns back to face him. "They'll probably want an explanation," he says, then clears his throat. "They'll want to know why you went off your meds. And to be honest, son, I'd like an explanation myself."

Danny's mom abruptly reaches out her hand and covers his father's hand. She pats it quickly, and Danny knows she's

trying to tell him it's going to be okay. They're in this together. Together they'll figure out a way to deal with their
freak son.

"Danny? We're waiting."

Danny's insides twist as he looks down at the bases of the
silver candleholders that are always in the center of the table.

You knew this was coming, he tells himself. *You knew you
were going to have to explain. You might as well get it over with.*

It's just that he can't stand this part—trying to make
them understand. They never have. And Danny's starting to
think he's going to have to accept the fact that they never
will. Still, if they want him to try, he has to try.

"I was just . . . I was *numb,*" Danny says, picking at his
fingernails. "I was walking around like a zombie. I kept falling
asleep. . . . I couldn't do my work. . . ." He lets out a frus-
trated sigh, feeling like he's not making any sense. "I can't
explain it. I didn't feel like myself. I didn't even feel human.
I couldn't take it anymore."

"And how you're feeling now is better?" his mother asks.

Sarcasm. Just what he needs right now. "No," he blurts
back. Then he remembers how frustrating it was to feel
nothing—not even anger or sadness or simple happiness.
"Maybe," he adds. "At least I'm feeling *something.*"

"But you can't live like this, Danny," his father says, his
eyes almost pleading. "You have to know that."

You do, a little voice in Danny's mind says as he looks
down again. *You know this depression won't last and then*

you'll be manic again. And you could hurt someone. Just like you did Abby.

"Yeah, I know," Danny says. He presses his palms into his eyes as the image of Abby just after the crash floods his mind. "I know. I went back on my medication, didn't I?"

"Yes, you did," his mother says. "But I still don't understand why you went *off* it without talking to us. You lied to us, Danny. You stood there and let us watch you swallow those—well, whatever it was you swallowed instead of your medication. You deliberately misled us. Why didn't you try to explain—"

"I did, Mom!" Danny snaps, surprising even himself. They both pull back a bit, stunned by the sudden outburst. Danny takes a deep breath and shakes his head, wondering where his body got the energy. "I tried to tell you . . . remember?" he continues, almost whining. "I told you I couldn't do my homework. That my new medication was messing with me. I told Dr. Lansky, but he kept saying I had to give it time."

His mother's face, ever so slowly, seems to register what he's saying. She starts to look ill.

"Daniel, don't blame your mother for your—"

"No, Joe, he's right. He did try to tell me," his mother says.

Danny is so surprised, he doesn't even know how to react.

"I'm sorry," his mother says, glancing up at him. "You did try to tell me."

For a moment Danny can't find his voice. What do you

say at a moment you've been waiting for all your life? His parents are actually listening to him.

It's about time, the little voice in his head says. *Why couldn't they have listened to you for the past seventeen years?*

Danny struggles to fight off a new wave of self-pity as this thought tries to pull him even further down. "It's okay, Mom," he says evenly. "I should have told you I wanted to go off my medication. I never told you that."

There's a collective deep breath at the table and they all look at one another, obviously unsure of how to proceed. But Danny has something to say, and if he can just make it come out, he hopes it will make his parents feel better. It may be physically impossible for *him* to feel better at the moment, but that doesn't mean he can't attempt to give them a little bit of hope.

"Look," Danny says, clearing his throat as he tries to push himself up again. "I just want to get better." His voice cracks and he feels a lump of sorrow well up in his throat, but he fights to keep it down. "I don't want . . . I don't want Abby and Jenny to be scared of me. That's not something I want. And I want you guys to be able to trust me. I think . . . I think the accident was like my wake-up call, you know? All I keep seeing is Abby and all that blood. . . ."

His mother covers her mouth quickly and he realizes she's been seeing it over and over as well. God, he hates himself for what he's done.

"I don't want to be this way," he says, sniffling. "I want to be better."

His parents slowly look at each other and they seem to deflate. It's like he can see any energy they had left seeping right out of them. Danny hadn't expected them to jump up and down, but he hadn't expected them to look defeated by his announcement, either.

"We'd love to believe you, Danny," his father says. "It's just—"

Danny squirms in his seat, not sure how much more he's going to be able to take.

"I know. I know I haven't given you any reason to trust me," Danny says desperately. "But please believe me, I'm going to try to get better."

He makes himself look them both directly in the eye. Tries to sound positive even though he's falling apart inside.

"You'll see," he says. "I'll do whatever it takes."

• • •

Sunday evening, Reed uses his third dinner roll to sop up the last drop of gravy from his plate. He stretches his arms out at his sides, full and satisfied. Reed can't remember the last time he didn't clean his plate. It had been one of his late father's strictest rules. Clean your plate or pay the consequences. Back then it was sometimes hard for Reed to get it all down, but these days he's getting down seconds and sometimes thirds.

"I suppose that means you enjoyed your meal?" Reed's mother asks, raising her perfect eyebrows with a small smile as he lets out a sigh of contentment.

"Yes, Mom," Reed says, leaning back in his seat. "It was great, as always."

"Yeah, Mrs. Frasier. You are an amazing cook," Jeremy chimes in, polite as always. Reed smiles across the table at his friend. He knows that Jeremy is truly grateful to him and his mother for letting him stay with them. No false compliments there.

T. J., who'd shown up that afternoon claiming he couldn't take one more college-cafeteria meal, groans as he stands up, lifting his arms above his head. "You outdid yourself, Mom," he says, walking behind her chair and planting a kiss on top of her coiffed blond hair. He places his large hands on her tiny little shoulders. "That's one of my favorite meals."

"That's why I made it," Reed's mother says. She reaches up to touch one of T. J.'s hands and smiles at him lovingly.

Reed glances over at T. J.'s vacated place. Not only are his plate and water glass still there, but the area around them is splattered with gravy and crumbs. A coil of tension curls its way through Reed's back and shoulders. He isn't sure why it bothers him that T. J. didn't clear his place. After all, he is categorically certain that T. J. has never cleared his own place in his life.

"I'm watching the Bills game in the den," T. J. announces as he makes his way out of the room without a second glance at the table. He stops just outside the door and turns, scratching at the back of his neck. "Oh, and don't hog the phone, guys. Karyn's gonna call."

Reed's heart seizes the moment T. J. says Karyn's name and he pauses halfway out of his chair, bracing his hands on the table. The hesitation only lasts a moment, though, and Reed pulls himself up straight, confident that neither his mother nor T. J., who's already turning on the TV in the den, even noticed. Jeremy, however, is trying very hard not to look at Reed as he clears his own dishes. Obviously his best friend caught his little heart palpitation. When is Reed going to get used to the fact that his brother and the girl who makes his pulse race are . . . intimate . . . in love?

All the blood rushes to Reed's face and he blurts out the first thing that comes to his mind. "Jeremy and I were going to use the den tonight," he says loudly so that T. J. can hear him in the next room. "We have to watch a documentary for a history project we're doing."

"Reed, I wish you wouldn't yell," his mother says as she pushes back her chair and stands. "If you want to talk to your brother, go into the den."

"Sorry, man!" T. J. calls back with a laugh. "First come, first served."

He turns up the volume on the television, obviously hoping that the sound of the roaring crowd and the nasal-voiced announcer will block out anything else Reed might have to say. Not that Reed would bother. He knows he'll get nowhere arguing his point. T. J., as always, will have his way in the end.

With a heavy sigh Reed picks up his plate as well as T. J.'s. Then he joins Jeremy at the sink.

"We'll just move my mom's VCR into my room and watch it in there," he tells Jeremy as he scrapes the dishes into the garbage.

"That's cool, man," Jeremy says with a nod. Reed feels his friend's eyes on him but decides to ignore it.

"Reed, don't forget to take out the garbage," his mother says as she hands Reed her own dishes.

Reed pauses once again and takes a deep breath but says nothing until she's safely out of earshot. As soon as he hears his mother's bedroom door close upstairs, he drops what he's doing with a clatter and walks over to the door between the kitchen and den. T. J. has the lights out and is sitting back on the couch with his feet up on the coffee table.

"Mom wants you to take out the garbage," Reed says, crossing his arms over the front of his Falls High football T-shirt.

T. J.'s eyes never leave the screen. "You do it, man," he says.

"It's your chore," Reed reminds him. Since T. J. comes home from school almost every weekend, he still has a few household chores—even if their mom seems to forget that.

"C'mon, man, I'm watching the game here," T. J. says, gesturing at the big screen TV.

Reed bites his tongue and rolls his eyes. "Fine," he says.

Back in the kitchen, Reed pulls the nearly full garbage bag out of the can and starts to gather up the bag at the top. Jeremy's eyeing him again, and this time Reed bites.

"What?" he says, looking up at Jeremy as he drops the bag on the floor in front of him and ties it off.

Jeremy seems to consider what he's about to say, concentrating on the pot he's scrubbing for a few extra seconds. Finally he shrugs and glances down at Reed.

"You can just tell me to shut up if it's none of my business," he says slowly. "But why do you let T. J. get away with that?"

"Get away with what?" Reed asks.

"Everything," Jeremy says firmly. "Ever since the guy's been home, you've practically been cleaning up after him. All he does is give you crap and you let him do whatever he wants."

Reed doesn't know how to respond. He knows Jeremy is right. Reed has been cleaning up after T. J. for years, and he's tried not to let it bother him. But hearing someone else say it makes it feel like a weakness. Like something he should somehow be ashamed of. If Jeremy knew what it was really like around here . . . But he couldn't. He wouldn't. Ever.

"You know what, man?" Reed says, his eyes flashing as he grabs the garbage bag. "Mind your own business."

Then he turns and heads out the back door to take care of T. J.'s chore.

● ● ●

By the time Jane returns to her mother's house on Sunday evening, she feels like she's about to collapse from exhaustion. Funny how not moving a muscle for two whole days can make a person feel like she's just run the New York Marathon.

Her mother opens the door before she gets there, just as she always does.

How did it go? Jane thinks, pushing through the door and dropping her book bag, duffel bag, and saxophone case on the floor. As she stands straight, she can feel all the tender spots where the straps cut into her shoulders.

"How did it go?" her mother asks.

"Fine," Jane says. *What did you eat?* her brain recites.

"What did you eat?" her mother asks. She crosses her arms and looks Jane up and down, apparently checking for signs of malnourishment.

"We ate fine, Mom," Jane says tonelessly. "All the food groups were represented."

What did you do?

"What did you do all weekend?"

Ah, a variation.

"Studied, mostly," Jane answers. She yawns and stretches, cracking her back, then leans down to pick up her bags.

"I have some stuff I have to finish, actually," Jane says, starting for the stairs. "I already ate, so . . ."

Her foot hits the first stair, then the second. As tired and heavy as she feels, Jane wills herself to move faster. If she can actually do it . . . if she can actually get up to her room before her mother starts in again, she could be safe for the duration of the night.

"I want to hear you practicing, Jane."

So much for that.

Jane places her sax and duffel bag down on the landing at the top of the stairs, turns, and sits down hard on the step just below freedom. Her backpack is so big, she's pushed all the way to the edge of the stair and has to brace her legs for balance.

"Mom, I have to write these pieces for the Web site—"

"They can wait," her mother says, looking up at her from the foot of the stairs, her small hand on the top of the wooden banister.

Jane sighs. She loves when her parents do that—tell her what can and can't wait as if they know what her deadlines are. Which test comes before which paper and how much practice she needs versus how much time she needs to study for an Academic Decathlon meet. She wonders if they realize how clairvoyant they make themselves sound.

"I know your father didn't make practicing a priority this weekend, so I have to," her mother continues. "It's important, Jane. Now more than ever. When those conservatories start calling to set up auditions, you have to be ready."

No one's going to be calling, Jane thinks. *I haven't applied.*

But her mother doesn't know that. No one does. And if her mother *did* find out that Jane has yet to fill out an application—if she found out *why*—Jane's way of life would be over. Neither one of her parents would ever look at her again.

All Jane is to her parents is her success, so she has to keep going. She has to keep making them think that she's still moving ahead. And moving ahead in two directions—one for him and one for her. Even if she's only moving ahead to nowhere.

"Jane, are you listening to me?"

Jane's eyes flick down and she looks at her mom. At her diminutive frame, the skin a few shades darker than her own, the tight jeans she's been wearing forever, the close-cropped hair that used to hang past her shoulders. Looking at her, Jane briefly remembers a time when she could tell her mother anything. When she'd sit next to her on the couch, talking about her day, the boy she had a crush on, the A she'd gotten in spelling.

Spelling. Had it been so long ago that she was still taking *spelling*?

"Jane? Are you all right?"

"Fine, Mom," Jane says, snapping herself out of her trance. The question may have been concerned, but there's nothing but accusation in her mother's brown eyes. Jane knows she's thinking that Jane's father worked her too hard over the weekend. That he made her study too much when she should have been playing her sax. Funny how her mother never thinks *she's* working Jane too hard.

Rising slowly, Jane knows that she should ask her mother about the Boston trip, but she doesn't have the energy.

"I have a lot of work to do, Mom," she says, then holds up a hand as she sees her mother opening her mouth to protest. "But don't worry, I'll practice."

She lifts her bags and trudges down to her bedroom,

mentally listing all the work she has yet to accomplish.

Study for AP bio, finish history paper, correct the specs for the Web site . . . practice for an hour. Keep on moving. . . . It's what you do.

Jane uses her foot to whack open the door to her bedroom, her shoulder to flick on the light. She takes one look at her desk chair and drops everything in her hands. There, where she'd neatly piled them, are three of the fifty or so college applications she'd requested over the summer. She'd promised Mrs. Carruthers, her guidance counselor, that she'd have at least three done by Friday. When she'd left for her father's two days ago, she'd figured she'd be finished with all her other work by now and have plenty of time to work on the applications, pointless as they are. Get them over with so she could spend the rest of the week studying for bio and preparing for the meet.

Rubbing her weary, cloudy eyes, Jane squints across the room at her alarm clock. The little red numbers are fuzzy around the edges, but she can read them. It's already nine o'clock. Jane slams her door behind her, tosses her sax case on her bed, and pops it open. First things first. And now that she is at her mom's house, that means one hour of practice.

The applications will have to wait.

CHAPTER THREE

"Okay . . . let's see," Jane mutters as she navigates her way through the crowded pre-homeroom halls on Monday morning. Her eyes are glued to the open notebook in front of her, so she's using her peripheral vision to dodge running freshmen, dropped books, and other potential hazards.

"Did that," she says, checking off the first item on the list of ten articles she either had to write or edit before today. Monday is the weekly deadline for all Web site articles to be in to the adviser and that means that if Jane doesn't have a piece in by now, she'll have to spend the rest of the day tracking down the writer, then somehow get the piece edited before the end of last period.

"Got that, did that, did that," she continues, a smile twitching at the corners of her lips with every item checked. There isn't anything that gives Jane more satisfaction than a completed to-do list.

"Reassigned that. Did that." Once she's done with this, she'll head to the lobby, pick up Peter Davis, get him to homeroom, and then go over her French homework. "Done!" Jane says, slapping the notebook closed with a smile.

"Jane! Jane! Wait up!"

Jane stops in the middle of the hallway, then slides over to the wall to let the hordes of people by. Glancing behind her, she sees Andrea Marra, a bucktoothed perfectionist who's in almost all of Jane's classes, bounding toward her. People move when they see Andrea coming, not because they're intimidated like they would be by a member of the elite like Reed Frasier or Gemma Masters, but because they know that if they don't move, Andrea will, unwittingly, flatten them.

"What's up?" Jane asks when Andrea finally reaches her, loudly breathless. "I'm kind of in a rush."

"I just wanted to find out what you got," Andrea says, her face flushed and her eyes bright with curiosity.

"What I got from what?" Jane asks, opening her hand in a gesture of cluelessness.

"On your SATs!" Andrea says in a "duh" tone. She holds up a little computer-generated piece of paper with the telltale leaf logo in the corner and Jane's knees almost give out from under her.

They're here. They're actually, finally here.

"You got your scores," Jane spits out. Her mouth is so dry, her tongue is sticking to the roof.

"Yeah! Why? Didn't you?" Andrea's pale face creases with disappointment. No, devastation. She obviously wanted to be the first one to find out what the great Jane Scott got on her college boards.

"No," Jane manages to say. She leans back against the cool cinder block wall, hoping that contact with something, anything, will keep her from passing out.

"Well, they'll probably come today, then," Andrea says, shrugging. She looks down at her own scores and her mouth twists up at the side. "I got a 1350: 650 verbal, 700 math." She shrugs again. "Not what I was hoping for, but I can always take 'em again, I guess. There's always January."

Take them again? Take them again? Jane feels like she's going to scream and vomit at the same moment. The girl got a 1350 and she wants to take them again. If she only knew . . .

There in the middle of the crowded hallway, with Andrea Marra breathing down her neck, Jane remembers with vivid clarity the empty Scantron page in front of her. Feels the sweat pouring down her neck and back. Sees her fingertips pressing into the pencil.

Take them again. Jane knows that she could, in fact, take them again as well. But just the thought of going through that once more causes her throat to dry out and close up with fear, making it difficult to breathe.

"I have to go," Jane says, the hallway starting to spin. "I have to find . . . Peter Davis. . . . You know . . . have to . . . go."

Andrea gives her a confused look, but Jane hardly notices. She quickly makes her way around the corner and back down the main hall, heading for the lobby on autopilot.

You'll just go home at lunch today and get your scores, she tells herself. *No one will ever know you were there. And once you have them, you'll figure out what to do. You'll have to.*

Jane takes a deep breath and tries to calm her racing thoughts, but she can't. After all this time, the nightmare is really coming true.

• • •

Okay, I was wrong. This *is what a parole hearing must feel like,* Danny tells himself on Monday morning. His legs are bouncing up and down uncontrollably under the table, but he's struggling to look normal from the waist up. If this meeting is going to go the way he needs it to go, he has to come off as normal.

Too bad I'm anything but, Danny thinks, pressing his sweaty palms into his thighs to try to stop his legs from moving. *Why am I here? I just want to get out of here. Why are they all looking at me like that? Can we go? Can we go? Can we go?*

Danny is seated at a large, round wooden table that's gleaming with fresh polish, with his parents on either side of him. His psychiatrist, Dr. Lansky, has just finished speaking. The man hadn't made Danny sound half bad, but the facial expressions on the rest of the meeting's attendees have not changed. The other chairs around the table are occupied by a rather large guy named Dr. Milewski-Brown from the Special Services department, Principal Maloney, Mr. Boyle, and Ms. Aufiero, Danny's guidance counselor. Every last one of them has that fake I-want-what's-best-for-you pinched smile on his or her face.

Except for his history teacher, Mr. Boyle—the guy he'd shoved in the incident that had landed him here. Mr. Boyle just looks disturbed.

Danny laces his fingers together, squeezing hard and trying to focus his mind away from his racing thoughts. *Sorry, Boyle, but you asked for it. You did and you know it. If I'd been on my meds, maybe I wouldn't have done it, but someone had to. . . .*

Danny's mother looks down at Danny's legs, reaches out, and puts a calming hand over his clasped ones. Taking a deep breath, Danny forces his speeding train of thoughts to shift tracks.

You know you shouldn't have pushed him. You know it was wrong. Calm the hell down. You have to get through this.

He presses his lips together, starts to count to ten in his mind.

"Thank you, Dr. Lansky," Principal Maloney, the head of festivities, says in his gravelly voice. "And you've directed Danny to go back on his medication?"

Yes, jerk-off, he has! Danny's brains screams.

Dammit! Deep breath. *One . . . two . . . three . . .*

"Yes, I have," Dr. Lansky says. "And he and his parents assure me that he's been taking his pills. Within a few days he should be stabilized."

"Fine . . . . fine," Mr. Maloney says, turning in his chair.

"Ms. Aufiero, is there anything you'd like to say before we get to Danny?"

Six . . . seven . . .

Every time Danny's name is spoken aloud, his stomach curls in on itself a little more. He's pretty sure that by the end of this meeting it will be so small, he'll never have to eat again.

Eight . . . nine—

"Yes. I've known Danny—in fact, the entire Chaiken family—for years," Ms. Aufiero says, aiming her bright, teenager-ish smile in the family's direction. "And I think we should all consider the fact that Danny is an extremely bright student. He's made the honor roll every year, he's very popular among the student body, and he participates in the jazz band and the drama club. He has been, barring recent events, nothing but a pleasure and an asset to this school."

A pleasure and an asset. Danny can't believe it. His face burns from the high praise that seems to come effortlessly from his guidance counselor. Who knew anyone felt that positively about him? His legs, for the moment, stop bouncing.

"I'm not saying he shouldn't be punished for his actions last week," Ms. Aufiero continues, "but I think it would be a detriment to the school if we were to expel him."

Both of Danny's parents shift in their seats as well and Danny can practically *feel* them trying not to smile. He's sure they're surprised and pleased by what Ms. Aufiero has said.

Maybe I have a chance, Danny thinks, his legs starting up

again. He leans forward in his chair, pressing his biceps hard against the edge of the table, and watches Principal Maloney scribble down a few notes. The pressure of the table against his arms feels good—grounding—so he pushes a little harder, hoping no one notices.

"Thanks, Ms. Aufiero," the principal says, capping his pen. He looks across the table at Danny and tucks his chin slightly, making sure he has Danny's full attention. "Now, Mr. Chaiken, Dr. Milewski-Brown and I would like to hear from you. What do you have to say for yourself about last week's incident?"

Even though Danny knew this moment was coming, his mouth goes dry the second he's called on to speak and his hands squeeze together even more tightly under the table. There's a chance that what he says right now will change the course of his entire future.

I can't do this. Not now. Not today. Why do I have to do this today?

His mother leans in to his ear and whispers, "Danny, sit back."

His heart pounds. So they did notice his intense posture. Damn. Damn. Damn. He knew it. There's no way they're going to take him back. Not when he's so obviously about to come out of his skin.

You have to do this. Take responsibility. It's the only way.

Danny takes a deep breath. He glances at Mr. Boyle, and Mr. Boyle just gazes back steadily. Clearing his throat, Danny looks up at his father, who nods almost imperceptibly.

You can do this, Danny thinks. *You have to.*

"Well, first off, I . . . uh . . . I want to say I'm sorry to . . . Mr. Boyle," Danny says, his voice sounding unusually loud in the small room. He flicks his eyes up at the teacher long enough to see the guy shift uncomfortably. "I don't know what I was thinking when I pushed you, and I want you to know that it'll never happen again. I mean it. I swear. I just got really angry, I guess, and I—" His mother touches his leg under the table and Danny freezes. He probably shouldn't have said that. Anger—snapping in anger—is not an image he wants these people to equate with him.

Dammit. I'm screwing up. Come on, Danny, focus. Focus, focus, FOCUS!

"But if I'd been on my medication, I wouldn't have done it. I know that." He says it so fast, it comes out like it's one word.

He looks over at Dr. Lansky, who gives him an encouraging smile. Danny doesn't know whether to smile back or hurl. On a normal day he can't stand Dr. Lansky, but he has to admit he's glad to have the guy here. At least the psychiatrist knows Danny's problems are real. That he's not just some delinquent who does this type of stuff on purpose to get attention or something. He knows how hard it is for Danny to even make sense when he's having a day like this one.

"Anyway, I am really sorry and I want to get better. I know what I have to do," Danny says, shoving his hands under his arms. "I don't expect you to believe me, but if you'll just give me a chance . . . I know I can be better."

The room falls silent and Danny swallows hard. The longer the quiet continues, the more hairs on Danny's arms and neck stand on end and the faster his legs move. He finally looks up at Maloney, who's watching Danny closely.

"That's it," Danny says. "That's all I've got."

Now hurry up and make a decision before I go insane, he thinks.

"Well, thank you, Danny," Mr. Maloney says with a kind smile. "I think that was very well put."

Yeah, if I was a kindergartener, Danny thinks. He glances at his mother and she doesn't look all that confident. In fact, she looks like she's ready to puke herself. Not the best sign. Danny wraps his arms a little more tightly around his torso.

"Mr. Boyle, I'd like to put you on the spot for a moment, if I may," Mr. Maloney says, turning to face the teacher. "Considering what you've just heard, would you feel comfortable having Mr. Chaiken return to your class?"

Danny's fingertips dig into his skin at his sides. Maloney's going to let *Boyle* decide his fate? The guy he laid out on the floor? The guy who has never made a reasonable decision in his entire teaching career? Danny might as well just leave right now and never look back.

The teacher looks at Danny, puffs out his cheeks, entwines his fingers in his lap. Basically, he takes his dear sweet time.

"Yes," Mr. Boyle says finally. "Yes, I believe I would."

Danny's breath catches in his throat. He has to be dreaming.

"Well, then, I believe we can all agree that a suspension will do," Mr. Maloney says quickly. "This is a first-time offense, there were obvious extenuating circumstances, and on most days Danny is, as Ms. Aufiero points out, one of our better kids. Finally, according to Dr. Lansky, Danny should be feeling fine again shortly." He slaps his folder closed and looks at Dr. Milewski-Brown. "Two days' suspension?" he says.

"And proof of prescription once his case has been reevaluated by his doctor," Milewski-Brown adds with a nod.

"That sounds fair to me," Mr. Maloney says. He smiles at Danny and his parents as he starts to rise from his chair. "Danny can return to school Wednesday."

Everyone starts to get up and Danny launches himself out of his chair, his muscles relieved that he's finally letting them move. Of course, now they want him to get up on the table and do a little dance of joy.

As his parents rise from their chairs and start to chat with the others, Danny stands there, his mind reeling. He's done it. He's gotten his second chance. For the first time since the accident, Danny actually feels a little light of hope inside him. If these people are willing to believe he can get better, then maybe he really can.

• • •

"Don't worry," Meena Miller says under her breath on Monday morning as visions of rotting lunches and undone homework assignments flit through her head. She takes a deep breath and pops open her locker, waiting for the pungent, nausea-inducing scent of moldy tuna. She can't remember the last time she actually bothered to go to her locker and she's sure it has to be gross.

But it's not. It is, in fact, as perfect and orderly and . . . cheery, as it's always been. Photos of Meena and her friends line the door, fastened by double-stick tape. There's a Falls High bumper sticker permanently attached to the side. Her books are all neatly stacked. Weird.

But then again, not so weird. Meena shakes her head at herself. Just because she feels like she's totally disheveled inside doesn't mean that everything else has fallen apart.

Glancing at herself in the tiny locker mirror, Meena is surprised by what she sees. There's actually some color in her cheeks, brought out by the light pink sweater she's wearing, and she doesn't look all bad. For the last few weeks she's worn nothing but grays, black, and browns, and she was starting to feel like the walking dead. The pink sweater is part of a deal she made with her therapist, Dr. Lansky. A deal she made partially in order to get him off her back and partially because she actually does *want* to feel better. And since she has no idea how to do that for herself, she figured she might as well try Dr. Lansky's way of doing things. It can't hurt, right?

So she's giving Lansky's plan a whirl. Aside from promising him she'll get up on time each day this week and eat something—even something small—four times a day, he also wanted her to try something new every day. Today's new thing is color. Not a bad choice.

Meena looks down at the bursting-at-the-seams duffel bag at her feet. Inside are her baggy blue sweatpants and a big, gray, zip-up-the-front sweatshirt. She left the house in them this morning and she'll be wearing them when she returns there again. Whenever that may be. Lansky's little deal won't solve everything. It won't take Steven out of her house. It won't erase everything that has happened. And the last thing she wants to do is show an inch of skin in front of Steven Clayton.

Clearing her throat, Meena tries to concentrate on the task at hand—remembering what her morning classes are. As she pulls down the books and loads up her backpack, she realizes that all in all, she does feel a bit better today. Steven had already been gone when she woke up this morning, so she'd been able to take a slow shower. And she'd even been hungry by the time she went downstairs, so she'd kept true to her deal with Lansky by eating a whole bowl of cereal. Ever since that monster breakfast on Sunday morning, she's been getting hunger pangs here and there for the first time in days. Apparently all those pancakes expanded her stomach.

Just as she's about to slam her locker shut, a voice cuts through her thoughts.

"Hey! So that's what your face looks like!"

Her cheeks darken as she turns to find Peter Davis smiling up at her.

"Not bad," he says, nodding.

Meena's hand self-consciously reaches back to touch the barrette that's holding her low ponytail, and she laughs.

Laughs.

It's been so long since she's heard that sound emanate from her own lips—so long since she's felt the sensation—that she immediately feels awkward. Like she's just screamed in the middle of the hallway and caught everyone's attention instead of merely giggling.

"Uh . . . thanks," she says, ducking her chin. Then she slams her locker closed and takes off down the hallway at a fast clip before he can say anything else. She has a feeling this blush is going to last long enough as it is.

• • •

Monday afternoon, Peter Davis is giddy. He's almost positive he's never *been* giddy before and he likes it. He likes the funny little tickly feeling in his chest that seems to somehow help suspend the goofy grin on his face. He likes the fact that nothing seems to bother him. Not the pity looks or the eye-contact dodgers or even the fact that he can't feel his body below the waist. It's unreal, actually.

"I really think I aced that test this morning," he says to Jane, who's pushing him at Mach speed through the hallway on their way to the cafeteria. "I mean, I've never had that feeling before, you know? That feeling like I actually knew everything on the test. I guess you get that all the time, right?"

Peter's met with silence and his heart drops as he remembers the last time he tried to speak to Jane about grades. She'd basically gone psycho all over him in the middle of the cafeteria. Feeling like an idiot, he braces himself for another tirade, but it doesn't come. He lifts his chin to look up at Jane. From the distracted look on her face, it seems possible that she didn't even hear him.

With a little relieved sigh, Peter sits back, folds his hands in his lap, and reflects on the morning. Jane's obviously in another one of her I'm-too-busy trances and that's fine by him. She can do whatever she wants. She can even ram him into another water fountain for all he cares. He's in a whole new place.

The first notch on his belt that day had been the history test in Boyle's class. Normally a history test would have been no cause for glee, especially not for Peter, who had never gotten above a C-minus in history in his life. But today had been different. Peter had spent the whole weekend studying for Boyle's exam. After the man had picked on him last week, causing Danny Chaiken to deck the teacher on his behalf, Peter had felt this nagging responsibility to kick ass on the exam and prove Boyle wrong about him.

At any rate, Peter had known almost every answer. He'd flown through the test. And with each new question he'd felt his heart lift just a little bit higher, felt himself sit up straighter in his seat.

Granted, Peter had already been psyched when he'd pulled his chair up to the desk to take the test. He'd been elated, actually. And all he'd done was make Meena laugh. The rush he'd gotten from seeing the normally morose, nearly catatonic girl giggle had been sensational. Maybe things were actually getting better for her. Maybe, in fact, things were going to start getting better for everyone. If Peter could have gotten out of his chair, he's pretty sure he would have jumped up and slapped the ceiling.

Peter stares up at the ceiling as it flies by him. Maybe one day . . .

Then, out of nowhere, he's spun around, and is suddenly being jerked backward.

"Hey!" Peter says, his head reeling.

"Sorry," Jane mutters, backing through the swinging doors into the cafeteria. She turns his chair once more and he's hurtling forward. The cafeteria is almost entirely deserted. They've gotten there so fast, no one is even at his table yet when she parks him at the end of it. Peter smiles, glad that his friends haven't arrived. It'll give him a few more minutes to relish his happiness. He knows that the moment the guys arrive, they'll ask him what he's so damn happy about, and if he tells them the truth, they'll proceed to pick on him until his high has been reduced to the lowest of lows.

Huh, Peter thinks as he comes to this realization. *Maybe I should sit with someone else.*

But he knows he won't. He's been hanging with Keith,

Max, and Doug forever. And as annoying as they can some-times be, it's still easier to sit with them than not to. He did sit with Jane once last week, but that didn't go so well. He's just going to have to suck it up and ignore his friends. Because he's not letting go of this feeling for anything.

"All right, I'll see you later," Jane says, fishing in her bag for her keys. She comes out with a large, unwieldy key chain and turns on her heel.

"Where ya going?" Peter asks brightly.

"That's really none of your business," she snaps.

Peter's face falls as he pops right out of his glee bubble. His heart turns at the close-to-crumbling look on Jane's face. "I'm sorry," he says. "Are you okay? I mean . . . what's wrong, Jane? You look—"

"You know, I got assigned to help you," Jane says, nar-rowing her eyes. "That does not mean we're going to be best friends." With that, she turns again and crosses the room in a flash, pushing through the glass doors that lead to the parking lot.

Peter watches her go, frowning. Something is seriously wrong with Jane. Maybe she's never been overly friendly, but last week they'd at least been able to have conversations with each other.

So maybe not *everything* is getting better. . . .

CHAPTER FOUR

"**I can't believe** I did that. I can't believe I'm such a bitch," Jane says to herself, speaking a mile a minute as she speeds through the rain-slicked streets of Winetka Falls. "I bit his head right off. Why don't I just shove the guy down a flight of stairs or something?"

But it's not her fault. She's been coming out of her skin all day, waiting for her lunch period so that she can go home and get the mail and hide her scores. It's not like she could have told Peter that. He'd just asked the wrong question at the very wrong time.

Jane is leaning forward in her seat, hunched over the wheel, eyes trained straight ahead as she drives. The windshield wipers are flapping back and forth at a psychotic speed, much too fast for the mere drizzle that's falling outside. Jane doesn't notice the squealing noise they make and is paying no attention to the road. She barely even registers the beeps and angry shouts she elicits from other drivers and pedestrians. There's only one thing on her mind. And contrary to what her mouth is rambling about, it's not Peter Davis.

Maybe they won't be there, she thinks, reaching over to flick on the car stereo and turning it up to an insane decibel. *Maybe they won't be there and everything will be fine.*

When her hand returns to the wheel, her fingers have crossed involuntarily.

"Please," she says softly, her heart pounding. "Please just don't let them be there."

But even as she says it, Jane knows this little prayer is pointless. If the scores aren't there—if by some miracle her prayer is answered—they'll just arrive tomorrow or sometime later in the week. She can't avoid this forever.

The closer Jane gets to her house, the more unhinged she becomes. Her palms sweat even though her hands are freezing.

Jane turns onto her street. The rain picks up as the car seems to steer its own way over to the curb. Jane slams on the brakes one moment before she would have flattened the mailbox entirely.

"Calm down before you do something stupid," she says to herself, flipping up the hood on her wool coat.

Shifting the car into park, Jane opens the door, starts to climb out, and is yanked back down by her seat belt. In a daze she reaches over and hits the button to release the belt. Then she gets out, letting the door swing open, groaning on its aging hinges.

Jane stands in front of the mailbox, squeezes her eyes

closed, and clenches her fists, hoping for some kind of miracle—just like she's done every day for the past couple of weeks. The SAT people made a mistake and gave her a 1400. They sent her a letter saying they've misplaced all answer sheets from the classroom she was in and because of their mistake are awarding everyone a perfect score. Or maybe, just maybe, they're simply not there.

Then, the daily mental ritual performed, Jane suddenly can't wait to look inside. She needs to feel that rush of empty relief she feels every time she opens the little door and is greeted by nothing but upscale catalogs and letters from random deans begging her to consider their schools. It's like a drug, that rush. A little shot of adrenaline that gives her one more day (and on Saturdays, two more days) to not deal with her parents.

She knows that today there's less of a chance that the mailbox will be score-free, but there *is* still a chance. Jane reaches up, swings open the door, and freezes.

The scores are there. Right on top.

The wide white envelope with the little blue leaf logo next to the return address. Raindrops fall off her hood like big, fat tears. Had the mailman known she was rushing home? Had he put these on top just for her? It's not like he doesn't know who she is. Everyone in this goddamn town knows who she is. And every one of them expects her to be this shining, perfect-grade machine.

Jane reaches into the box, grabs the envelope, rips it

open, and pulls out the sheet, hands shaking. And there they are. Just as they have been in all of her nightmares for the last few weeks. 100 verbal. 100 math. The score you get for signing your name. Raindrops hit the page, making the paper translucent.

Jane laughs.

Her hand claps over her mouth and her eyes fill with tears, but she can't stop laughing. It's all too ridiculous. Her parents had practically locked her in her room every single day for her entire junior year, forcing her to study vocabulary lists, math problems, practice test after practice test. It was almost the only thing they had agreed on since their divorce—the importance of her scores.

They'd debated about how much her numbers would improve after the sorry showing of 1300 on her PSATs. 1300. Not whether they would improve, but *how much* they would improve. And 95 percent of her class would have *killed* for a 1300. Would have maimed, ravaged, and pillaged. Would have ransomed their firstborn sons!

For one scary, euphoric moment, Jane imagines telling her parents the news. She envisions herself inviting her father over and bringing them both into the living room. Sees herself pulling the scores out of her jacket pocket and placing the paper down in front of them. Sees their faces going slack.

And then, her heart slamming an erratic beat in her ears, Jane hears herself say the words she's been trying to avoid even thinking about since the day of her SATs. She hears the words and lets them sink into her brain for the first time. Lets reality take hold.

I'm not going to college. I'm not going to a conservatory. And there's nothing you can do about it.

Jane clenches her jaw, making herself believe this truth. And in that one fleeting moment, she knows she can do it. She doesn't care if they disown her. She doesn't care if they're disappointed. There's nothing they can do about these scores. Now is the time. It's staring her in her rain-slicked face.

She can't lie anymore. It's time to finally face reality.

Fingers fluttering, Jane folds the sheet of paper in half, then in fourths, then eighths, then squeezes the crease between her fingers and shoves the little square in the back pocket of her jeans. She takes the maimed envelope and does the same, pushing it into the other back pocket. After carefully closing the mailbox, Jane returns to the still running car and sits down sideways on the front seat, her feet still on the ground outside.

She's going to have to do it. She's going to have to confront her parents. And at that one simple thought in the midst of all the confusion in her mind, Jane bends her face toward her knees and quietly starts to cry.

● ● ●

"I don't believe it. We got exactly the same score," Reed says into the phone on Monday evening. He holds his SAT scores in his hands as he cradles the receiver between his shoulder and cheek. He hasn't stopped grinning since he opened the envelope an hour ago. He'd known he was going to do well, but *this* well?

"Almost the same," Sumit says on the other end of the line, sounding just as psyched as Reed feels. "I'm the math brain and you're the wordsmith, apparently."

"Yeah, except I'd never use a word like *wordsmith* in an actual sentence," Reed says, laughing.

Across the room Jeremy chuckles and shakes his head as he watches some sitcom rerun on Reed's TV. Reed glances at him and Jeremy rolls his eyes. It's obvious he's laughing at Reed's pure and utter dork factor and not at the stupid antics of the family on the screen.

"Sumit, I gotta go," Reed says.

"You're gonna call Jane, aren't you?" Sumit asks.

Reed shifts in his seat and puts his scores down on his desk. "I would, but she's working at TCBY this afternoon," he says, lifting his baseball cap from his head and scratching his fingers through his hair.

"What time does she get home?" Sumit asks. Reed can practically *hear* him salivating.

"She gets off at six," Reed says with a laugh. "But give her a few seconds to get the mail before you call her, all right?"

The moment Reed hangs up the phone, Jeremy flicks off the television. "I don't believe you, man," he says with a smirk. "You already *called* Jane and left her a message."

"I know," Reed says, leaning back in his chair and splaying

his long legs out in front of him. "I want her to call me before she talks to Sumit."

Jeremy tilts his head and narrows his eyes at Reed.

"What?" Reed asks, lacing his hands together behind his head.

"I'm just now noticing what a total dork you are," Jeremy says matter-of-factly. "How could this have escaped my attention before?"

"Whatever," Reed says. Reed's always been rather proud of his academic ability. It sets him apart from the crowd. There are jocks, and there are brains, but at Falls High there are very few people who straddle the line. "Do you want to run home and see if your scores came?" he asks Jeremy.

"You couldn't pay me to go home right now," Jeremy says, picking up the remote and turning the TV on again. "Besides, it doesn't really matter what I got. If it's anything like my PSAT scores, it'll be enough to get me into one of the SUNYs."

Reed laughs and tips forward in his chair, leaning his elbows on his knees. "How do you do that?" he says. "How can you completely not care? I've been waiting for these things for weeks."

"I'm not an honors student," Jeremy says with a shrug. "You guys are more competitive with each other than—"

"Hey! What're we talking about?" T. J. interrupts, sticking his head into Reed's room. "Reed and his troop of brainiacs?"

Reed feels his face flush and he moves a folder on his desk to cover the letter from the College Board.

"You know, Mandile, sometimes I can't believe Reed and I are even related," T. J. says, moving farther into the room and crossing his arms over his sizable chest. "I mean, do you really think it's possible that I share the same blood as someone who is clearly such a huge loser?"

As T. J. laughs at his own joke and Jeremy shoots Reed a sympathetic look, Reed feels his blood start to boil. He hears Jeremy's words from the day before. *All he does is give you crap and you let him do whatever he wants.*

"Kiss my ass, T. J.," Reed blurts out, glaring up at his brother.

"Ooh! Doesn't the brain have anything better than that?" T. J. says, waggling his fingers in front of him as he continues to laugh.

"Right, I'm the loser," Reed says. "Shouldn't you be in class right about now?"

"No," T. J. says, the smile finally waning from his features. "My Monday class was canceled. And since when are you my keeper, anyway?"

Yeah, right, Reed thinks. *I know you're just skipping because you can't handle it.*

"That's great," he says, looking up at T. J. "Maybe if they cancel enough classes, they'll have to give everyone an A. It's about the only chance *you* have of passing a college-level class."

Reed freezes as T. J.'s face turns so red, it's almost purple. He can practically *see* his own words piercing his brother's chest.

66

T. J. glances at Jeremy, obviously humiliated. "Whatever," he says to Reed. "Just . . . whatever." He walks out and slams the door so hard that Reed's framed picture from last year's junior prom falls off the wall and crashes onto his desk.

"I can't believe I did that," Reed says, feeling like something inside him is breaking.

"He deserved it," Jeremy says. "He was all over you."

"Yeah, but the one thing I never do is mock T. J. about his grades," Reed says. He rubs his face with both hands and takes a deep breath. Slumping back in his hard-backed chair, shoulders forward, Reed looks at Jeremy. He's never told anyone this, but Jeremy's living here now. He might as well have a little bit of insight into the dysfunction that is the Frasier family.

"T. J. has dyslexia," Reed says quietly. Jeremy's head moves back a bit and he blinks, taking this in. "School's always been really hard for him." Reed blows out a sigh and shakes his head. "I'm such a jerk. I can't believe I said that." His heart twists in his chest, making it difficult to breathe.

Jeremy mutes the TV and moves to the edge of the bed, sitting forward. "Look, I understand how you feel. But T. J.'s doing fine now. He's at a good school. . . . Having dyslexia doesn't give him the right to be an asshole all the time."

"You don't understand—"

"What, is he jealous that you're smart?" Jeremy asks, his face screwing up with indignation. "He was born one way and you were born one way. It's not like you have any control

67

over the situation. I mean, you don't have to take that crap from him. You don't owe him anything because you're a brain."

Reed clasps his hands together tightly, watching his fingertips turn red from the pressure. Jeremy doesn't get it. Reed owes T. J. everything. And not because he's smart and T. J. is dyslexic. He owes his brother for a million other reasons. But Jeremy can't possibly know that, and he never will. Reed suddenly feels the need to get out of this conversation as quickly as possible.

"You're right," he says. "Screw him." Reed forces an empty smile, which seems to satisfy Jeremy.

"Exactly. Screw him," he says. He turns the volume back up on the TV and sits back again.

Reed turns and pulls out his scores again, staring down at them and trying to gather back some of the elation he'd felt a few minutes ago. But it's all gone. He can't even remember what it felt like. All he can see is T. J.'s humiliated expression. And all he can feel is guilt.

• • •

"Okay, this is depressing me," Danny says to himself, slamming his book shut and flinging it like a Frisbee across his room. "You'd think that if you were going to write a book for manic-depressives, you'd at least make it a little bit upbeat, but *nooooo*."

He slumps back into his pillows and glares at the small heap of books lying on the floor. He'd taken them out of the library so that he could read up on his disorder—try to educate himself so that he'd know how to get better.

And he'd been educated, all right.

"I'm going to be a single, alcoholic, jobless, suicidal loser," Danny mutters. A picture instantly flashes into his mind of himself, balding and paunchy, drinking a beer in some run-down shack, contemplating different ways to off himself.

A little cloud of self-pity starts to roll in over Danny's shoulders and he can feel it weighing him down, pressing him into the bed.

"No!" he says, standing up. He kicks the books out of the way, walks over to his stereo, and flicks it on, cranking up the sound. He is not going to let himself mope. There will be no going to dark places. Everything is going to be fine.

Danny pauses in the center of his room and stuffs his hands under his arms, pinching at his sides. Where was that little twinge of hope he'd felt that morning? It couldn't be gone already, could it? He'd really liked that sensation. That lightness. So why now, only hours later, is it impossible to remember?

I should never have read those books, Danny thinks, scrunching his eyes closed. *I could have at least skipped those sections about potential problems. I'm so stupid. I should have known those statistics would freak me out. I'm like a masochist or something.*

Once Danny had seen that people with his disability

69

had greater chances of falling into destructive patterns, he'd pretty much forgotten every positive thing he'd read. Anything about strides made with medication and therapy, any statistics about people who *did* succeed, went right out of his mind.

"I'm going to be fine," he tells himself, pacing his room. "I'm not gonna be an alcoholic or a drug addict or an abusive father. I'm not. It's not me. It's not me. It's not me. . . ."

But the more he says it, the less true it feels. There is something wrong with him. All the books say it. Something wrong in his brain. How can he compete with that? How can he fight against the inevitable?

• • •

Monday evening, Jane trudges into her darkened house, exhausted. The emotional roller-coaster ride she'd been on all day had taken every last ounce of energy out of her, and a long shift at TCBY had sucked out what was left of her second wind. But at least her mom isn't home yet. Maybe she can just get a few minutes to herself to breathe. Or maybe her mother has a parent-teacher night at the middle school where she teaches. Maybe she won't be home for hours.

The thought makes Jane smile as she closes the door behind her, even though she knows there's no such event this evening. Her mother always lets her know exactly where she's going to be, just as she expects to always know exactly where Jane is. At least there's no double standard there.

Turning on the hall lights, Jane makes her way to the

kitchen and sure enough, there's a note in the middle of the table. *At the supermarket. Be back soon!*

She's about to head upstairs to shower off the sticky sheen of yogurt that somehow always seems to cover her arms after a shift, that when she notices that the little red light on the answering machine is blinking. Jane hits the button and hovers over the machine.

"Hey, Jane! It's Reed. I know you're working this afternoon, but I got my scores and I just wanted to see if you got yours. Sumit and I are dying to see what you got. I know you probably blew us outta the water, but, you know. Just . . . call me back."

Jane flinches. He obviously did well. Very well. She's about to listen to the message again, just to confirm the sickening suspicion, when she hears her mother's key in the back door lock. Jane quickly hits the delete button. The tape rewinds and the three beeps sound to confirm that the message has been erased just as Jane's mother pushes through the door, her arms filled with bags, her pocketbook dangling from her wrist.

"Hey! You need help?" Jane asks, bounding across the room. She takes both bags from her mother as the phone rings, abruptly stopping Jane's heart.

"Thanks, sweetie," her mother says, pulling the strap of her shoulder bag back up. "I'll get it."

"No, it's okay," Jane says as she fumbles the bags onto the table. She has to get to the phone first. "I'll—"

But her mother is already there. Jane's pulse is racing so

fast, she's sure she's about to have a heart attack or an aneurysm or something that will land her in the hospital. Not such a bad idea, actually. At least it would take the focus away from other things.

"Hello? Oh, hello, Sumit." Her mother glances at her, smiling. "Yes, she's right here. Hold on."

She holds the phone out to Jane, who has to walk slowly to prevent her knees from buckling. She takes the phone in her sticky, sweaty hands and brings it to her ear.

"Hey, Sumit," she says, aware that her mother is watching her closely. Ms. Scott knows Jane's scores should be coming any day now. It's just one of the drawbacks of having a mother who is part of the educational system.

"Hey, Jane," Sumit says. He's practically bubbling with giddiness. "You know why I'm calling, so just tell me. Whadja get?"

Jane clears her throat, shifts her weight from one aching foot to the other, loops her finger through the coiled phone cord. Lies.

"I, uh, didn't," she says. "They didn't come."

Her mother's face falls as Sumit sucks in his breath.

"Aw, *man!*" he says. "You're kidding. I wanted to rub your face in my superiority."

Jane forces a scoff as Sumit would expect. "Whatever." There's a silence and Jane swallows. She knows he's waiting for her to ask him. There's just no way around it. "So . . . what did you get?"

"Well, it hardly seems fair to tell you when you have nothing to share, but of course I will," Sumit says. "I got a 1440. 740 math, 700 verbal. Ha! Top that, Ms. Valedictorian."

There are no words in Jane's head. Odd, considering her mind is usually racing on about four different tangents. She pulls a chair over to her and sits down, wiped all over again. She doesn't even care that her mother is standing there, watching her every move.

"Jane?" Sumit says. "Did you hang up or are you just too awestruck to speak? 'Cuz, you know, I'd understand either reaction."

Finally Jane remembers how to talk. "Awestruck, I guess," she says. "That's great, Sumit. Congratulations."

"Thanks," Sumit says, still preening. "I'm sure yours will come tomorrow, and then we'll see just how badly I smoked you."

If you only knew, Jane thinks, an incongruous smile twitching at her lips.

"Jane?" Sumit says, his tone more subdued. "I'm sorry. You know I'm just kidding."

"I know."

"Kind of," he jokes.

"I know," she says again. She takes a deep breath. "I gotta go, Sumit. I'll see you tomorrow. And really, congratulations."

"Thanks, J.," Sumit says. "Later."

The moment Jane hangs up the phone, her mother is ready and waiting.

"Sumit got his scores and you didn't?" she says, her eyebrows knitting together as she unpacks the groceries. "That's odd, isn't it?"

Jane stands and pushes her chair back under the table. "I guess," she says with an elaborate shrug. "I don't know how it works." She studiously avoids looking her mom directly in the face. If she does, her cover will be blown. She's sure that after the day she's had, her emotions have to be written all over her.

Why don't you just do it? a little voice in Jane's mind asks. *You know you have to. Time to face reality, remember?*

But she can't. There's no way. Her mother will be so disappointed. No, devastated. Jane can't even imagine the way her mother will look at her when she finds out the truth, but she knows she won't be able to handle it. She can't do it yet. Not yet.

Tears sting at the corners of Jane's eyes as she busies herself with unpacking the other bag. She walks into the spacious pantry with a couple of cans of soup and hesitates there for as long as possible. *She's going to know you're lying. She's going to know.*

"So he did well, I assume," Jane's mother prompts.

"Yep," Jane calls.

Change the subject, Jane. Talk about something else. Anything. Anything distracting. She racks her brain. What? What could possibly steer her mother away from the subject of the SATs? Then, like a flash of brilliance, it hits her.

"Mom? Dad wants to take me to Boston to visit MIT

this weekend," Jane says, emerging from the pantry.

Her mother stands in the middle of the kitchen, a bag of bread in one hand, a box of dish detergent in the other. Her eyes are so wide, Jane immediately thinks of a Saturday morning cartoon she used to watch as a kid.

"He *what?*"

Jane winces. Dogs miles away probably heard that screech.

"MIT and Boston College and Harvard," Jane says quietly, placing her hands on the back of a chair.

"Who does he think he is?" Jane's mother shouts, slapping the bread and detergent box down onto the counter. She turns to Jane, hands on the hips of her long flowy skirt. "He doesn't even have you this weekend! Did he even think of that?"

"I know, Mom," Jane says, the muscles in her shoulders coiling. "I guess he didn't think—"

"Exactly! He didn't *think!* Does he *ever* think?" Her mother is rapidly losing it now, gesturing wildly with her hands with every exclamation. "Did he even ask you if you *wanted* to visit those schools? Did it occur to him to consider Boston Conservatory or Berklee? Noooooo . . ."

And there it is. The real reason for the tirade. Jane watches as her mother grows more and more agitated, speaking to no one now. She picks up the phone and starts to dial Jane's father's number, shouting all the while. The moment Jane's father picks up the phone, her mom laces into him. No hello. No pleasantries. All yelling.

With a heavy sigh Jane walks past her mother and heads upstairs to her room.

They were going to have this fight anyway, she reasons. *There was nothing you could do to stop it.*

Closing her door behind her, Jane sinks down on her bed, mentally running through all the work she has to do tonight. This week. This month. This marking period.

Don't do it. Don't bother, the little voice chides. *There's no point.*

Jane pulls the scores out of her back pocket and stares at them. She still can't believe they're here. Still can't believe there's actual physical proof of her failure.

"But they don't know," Jane says to herself.

Sooner or later they're going to find out. All Jane can do is make sure that it's later.

CHAPTER FiVE

Tuesday morning, as Jane pushes Peter's chair through the bustling hallway toward his second-period class, she has to grip the handles tightly to keep herself from screaming. If one more person asks her what she got on her SATs, she's pretty sure she'll be the first case of spontaneous combustion in New York State history.

"Jane! Wait up!"

Jane merely pushes faster. Everyone around her seems to be holding a score sheet, going over them with their friends, looking at Jane and whispering about what she must have gotten. People Jane barely even knows have asked her about her scores. Why can't everyone just leave her alone?

Edging ever closer to an explosion, Jane quickly turns a corner and, in her rush to get away from her newest inquisitor, accidentally runs Peter's chair into the back of Karyn Aufiero's leg.

"Ow!" Karyn protests, wheeling around to yell at whoever has smashed into her. But the moment she sees Peter, her face turns all red. She pauses for a second, a strange, distracted expression on her face, and then, clearly uncomfortable, she hurries off down the hallway.

"You okay?" Peter asks Jane when the coast is clear.

"Fine," Jane says tersely.

At that moment Sumit and Reed walk out of the bathroom and stop right in front of Jane and Peter. When they see Jane, they exchange a knowing look and then Reed crosses his arms over his chest, indicating that he won't be moving anytime soon. Jane's jaw clenches and she gives them her best glare, but they just look at her with matching smiles.

"Hey, Peter," Reed says, curling the brim of his baseball cap with one hand. "So . . . Jane, Sumit says you haven't gotten your scores yet."

"Nope. Haven't gotten 'em," Jane confirms. She backs Peter's chair up a notch, then shifts it right to go around her friends. They don't take the hint, however, and decide to just follow along. Jane can feel her shoulders pulling in under her backpack. These are some of the smartest guys in the school. How can they possibly miss all of her go-away signals?

Maybe they'll leave me alone when we get outside, she thinks. Lately she's been taking Peter through the courtyard to get to the other end of the building because there are fewer people out there when it's freezing. She'd started doing it because she didn't have to maneuver his chair as much, but fewer people also meant fewer questions. Added bonus.

"See, man?" Sumit says as the two guys fall into step on either side of Jane. "I told you."

Reed cracks a half smile as he holds the door at the end of the hall open for Jane and Peter. "Know what I think?" he says, smirking at Jane as she walks by into the courtyard. "I think you're just too nice. I think you got your scores and you just don't want to rub our noses in them."

Jane lets out an involuntary laugh. If only she'd somehow gotten scores worthy of a nose-rubbing. Jane knows she definitely wouldn't refrain from a little gloating if she were in the position to do so.

"You guys, I have a lot to do," Jane says, staring straight ahead as the cold air hits her face. "I swear if I get my scores, you will be the first to know."

"We'll hold you to that," Reed says good-naturedly as he and Sumit turn and head back in the other direction.

I'm sure you will, Jane thinks. She knows Reed and Sumit are nice guys and they don't mean to be pushing her to the brink of a meltdown, but that doesn't make the feeling of suffocation any more bearable.

Then, before she can even force herself to breathe, Andrea Marra appears out of nowhere, her face bright with excitement. "Hey, Jane! Did you get your—"

"No!" Peter blurts out, half shouting. "She hasn't gotten her scores, okay?"

Jane stops in the middle of the courtyard, stunned, while Andrea loses all color in her face. It seems to flow directly into her ears, which turn bright red just before Andrea blurts out an apology and pushes through the double doors back into the school.

A stiff breeze kicks up and blows a few dead leaves across the ground as Jane simply stands there, breathing in and out. The edge has been taken away slightly. Just slightly.

"I can speak for myself, you know," Jane says, in a tone that is firm but still retains a thank-you.

"I know. I just thought you could use a guard dog there," Peter says with a shrug. Jane turns his chair and wheels him back into the school. "Besides, I'm getting sick of hearing the question, too, you know? I do happen to be with you most of the day."

Jane sighs. He has a point. But even if he does have to endure all the questions, he can't possibly know how it feels. Of course, she *had* given him a bit of a taste yesterday when she'd bitten his head off for no apparent reason.

"Listen, I'm sorry about snapping at you yesterday," Jane says, coming to a stop in front of Peter's classroom. "I just have a lot going on."

"Don't worry about it," Peter says. He reaches down and pulls at his left wheel so that his chair turns around and he's facing Jane. He looks up at her with a kind, patient expression in his green eyes and Jane instantly feels her chest tighten. If one more muscle in her body winds up, she's going to be a human-sized ball.

"If you ever want to talk about it . . . ," Peter says, tilting his head slightly.

"Thanks, but I'm fine," Jane answers. It's nice of Peter to offer, but the last thing she wants to do is talk about everything.

I just want it to all go away, she thinks. *I just want it to stop.*

Then, before she gives in to the tears that are threatening to spill over, she turns and pounds her way through the doors, back out into the courtyard. As soon as the cool air hits her, the tears disappear and Jane stops, hugging herself against the chill.

What is wrong with her? Why did she almost start crying back there? Has it been so long since anyone's bothered to listen to her that the mere gesture actually brings her to tears?

"Get a grip. Everything is going to be fine," Jane lies to herself, glancing at her watch.

The warning bell rings and Jane takes off for her English class, where she'll have to finish her calc homework while taking notes and then work on an article revision for the Web site. She has to keep it up. Keep up the facade. As long as she keeps doing her work, there will be fewer questions. Less of a chance that someone will figure out the truth. Figure out that she's a fraud. A failure.

• • •

Danny can't breathe. Something is holding him down. He pushes and pushes and finally, whatever it is rolls off him and the moment the oxygen hits his lungs he hears laughter. The laughter of little kids. Danny tries to get up, but when

81

he lifts his head, Reed Frasier tackles him to the ground. They roll over on the hard, carpeted floor. And now Danny's laughing, too. There's nothing to be afraid of. It's just a game.

Somebody grabs his ankles and he looks down to see Karyn Aufiero, pigtails tangled and mussed, grinning as she pulls off his shoes. She jumps on top of Reed and they all tussle. Pulling and pushing and tumbling.

"Danny . . . Danny . . . Danny . . ."

As soon as he hears his name being called, a chill grips Danny. Who is it? What do they want?

"Danny . . . Danny . . . Danny . . ."

"Get off me! Get off me, Reed!" Danny shouts. Reed just keeps laughing and playing and Danny finally shoves his way free. He stands up, sweaty and disheveled, and sees Peter Davis sitting in his wheelchair, holding Danny's little sisters' hands. They stand on either side of the chair in matching outfits and all three of them chant his name.

"Danny . . . Danny . . . Danny's fault, Danny's fault, everything is Danny's fault. . . . Danny's fault, Danny's fault, everything is Danny's fault. . . ."

"No!" Danny shouts, tears springing to his eyes. "Stop it! Stop it! I don't want to hear any more!"

But they just keep droning on. "Danny's fault, Danny's fault, everything is Danny's fault. . . . Danny's fault, Danny's fault, everything is Danny's fault. . . ."

"Shut up!" Danny shouts, getting right in Peter's face. "Shut up! Shut up!"

It's as if they don't even hear. They just keep chanting and chanting until Danny feels like he's going to explode. Then out of nowhere, there's a deafening bang—

Danny wakes up and gasps for air. Bleary-eyed and completely confused, he looks around the room, his heart trying to pound its way through his rib cage. It takes him a full ten seconds to realize he's in his own living room. It's Tuesday. The middle of the afternoon. He's perfectly safe. Suspended from school, but safe.

He looks at the clock and realizes he's been asleep for about an hour. He'd just passed out. Does that mean his meds are kicking in again? Is the whole foggy, groggy, sleepy thing starting up again? Or had he just been bored and tired and fallen asleep like any normal person would have in the face of nonstop game shows and soap operas?

Danny hates the fact that he doesn't know the answers to these questions.

The doorbell rings and nearly scares Danny right out of his skin. He jumps up and kicks the throw blanket away from his ankles, then rushes over to the door.

He opens the door, yawning and scratching his chest, and then almost slams it shut again. It's Cori Lerner. She looks perfect. And he's wearing his pajamas.

"Hey, Danny," she says, looking him up and down. "Killer threads. You get dressed up just for me?"

Why, oh, why didn't I change when I got out of bed this

morning? Danny laments. He hasn't even brushed his teeth today, and he's sure there are sleep creases all over his face. In the many fantasies he's had about Cori showing up at his house, he's never been wearing a Star Wars T-shirt and a pair of flannel boxers. He's never been sitting out a day because of a suspension.

"Hey," he says. There isn't a single joke or witty comeback in his half-asleep mind. "What are you doing here in the middle of the day?" he asks.

"Well, I was just on my way back to school after lunch and I thought I'd stop by and tell you we have a test in English on Friday," she says.

"Gee . . . thanks," Danny says sarcastically. "You woke me out of my beauty sleep for that?"

Cori laughs, her bright blue eyes sparkling, and Danny's heart responds with a little extra thump. "Well . . . I was *thinking* . . . since you haven't been in class the last couple of days, you might want to come by and get my notes tonight and . . . you know . . . study."

Danny's mind is racing. Was there a suggestion in that little invitation? No. No. Not possible. Cori Lerner is not interested in him. The gods are not that kind. She's just being helpful, that's all. But just her presence here means she isn't freaked out by what happened in class last week. She isn't going to disown him because he snapped and made a scene and got suspended.

"Sounds good to me," Danny says. He shuffles his feet, shifting his weight from one leg to the other, embarrassed about what he's going to say. "I have to clear it . . . you know . . . with my parents first," he says, looking down at his hole-filled socks.

"Well, convince them it's for your own academic good," Cori says as a breeze lifts her straight black hair off her neck and tosses it around, the red highlights gleaming in the sun. "You can come over around seven . . . but you should probably clean yourself up first." She leans over and peels something off Danny's sleeve, then holds it up in front of him. It's a fruit-roll-up wrapper. Cherry.

If I'm ever going to get struck by lightning, please let it happen now, Danny thinks, his face burning.

"Uh . . . I think I can manage that," he says. Cori didn't have to do this. She didn't have to come by here and offer her help. It's like every time he sees her, she gives him another reason to pine for her.

"Cool," Cori says with a grin that makes his whole body respond.

"Cool," Danny repeats.

Cori crosses her arms over her black leather jacket and studies him for a moment and suddenly Danny knows what's coming. She's going to ask him about Boyle. About the accident. About the suspension. And he doesn't have the answers. At least, he doesn't have any answers that he'd want her to hear.

She opens her mouth to speak, and Danny cuts her off.

"So, I guess everyone at school thinks I'm a psycho, huh?" he asks. Not that he cares. All he cares about at that moment is whether or not Cori thinks he's a psycho.

She laughs a quick, dismissive laugh. "It *was* insane, watching you flatten Boyle like that," she says, causing Danny's stomach to contract. He still can't believe she'd been in the room. That he'd let her see him like that. Not that he'd had much control over himself at the time.

"But I think everyone wishes they'd done it first, you know?" Cori continues, hugging her jacket closer as the wind picks up. "I mean, *I* wanted to smack him for the way he was talking to Peter."

A little smile pulls at Danny's mouth. She understands. Well, she doesn't *totally* understand because she doesn't know the whole under-the-surface story, but she agrees with him. Maybe he hadn't looked like such a psycho after all.

"I heard you were in an accident, too," Cori says, her brow furrowed.

"Yeah," Danny says flatly. "Some weekend."

"Seriously," Cori shoots back. "What happened?"

"Oh . . . well . . ." Danny tucks his hands under his arms, leans into the doorjamb, racks his brain. What's he supposed to tell her? *Well, I was having a manic episode, and I was driving like I was on speed. You understand.*

Yeah, right.

"It was my sisters," he lies. "They were . . . you know . . . fighting and I . . . I had to turn around to get them to stop, so I wasn't watching the road and . . . you know . . . that's pretty much it."

"Wow," Cori says. "But everyone's okay?"

She's buying it, Danny thinks with a mixture of guilt and relief.

"Yeah, everyone's fine," he answers, quickly blocking out the image of Abby that once again threatens to flood his mind.

"Well, I guess they won't be fooling around in the car again anytime soon," Cori says lightly.

"Shyeah," Danny says, snorting a laugh. Suddenly, as much as he wants Cori to stay and hang out with him forever, he needs her to go. He can't handle lying to her like this. The longer she stands there, the more he hates himself.

"Well, I'd better get back," she says, twisting her shoulders toward her car. Danny tries not to look relieved. "Call me when you know for sure about tonight."

"I will," Danny says.

She heads back down the path and ducks into her car, then smiles and lifts her hand in a wave before she drives off.

Danny closes the door and leans back against it, letting out a heavy sigh. He wants to see her tonight so badly. But he's not sure he can handle more questions, more lying, more guilt and self-loathing. As Danny returns to the living room, his brain starts to race, going over everything he's just said, what he'll say when he asks his parents, what he and Cori will do if he does get to go over there tonight.

By the time he hits the couch again, he can't block out the loud, mind-bending race of thoughts.

Danny squeezes his eyes shut and sinks down on the couch, trying to regain control of his brain. And finally one thought starts echoing louder than the rest—*No. The meds haven't kicked in again yet.*

• • •

Reed can't pull his eyes away from his brother's. Granted, they're not his brother's *real* eyes—they're his eyes in a black-and-white photo that's hanging inside a glass case in the hallway at school. Only a select few have been immortalized in the trophy case outside the gym, and his brother is one of them. He is, in fact, the most prominent one, with his Athlete of the Year picture front and center in the case, surrounded by a framed article and a couple of trophies. Reed usually walks right by the trophy case without a second glance, but today, for some reason, he can't move away from it.

The door to the locker room opens and Jeremy walks out. Reed glances at him, then returns his eyes to T. J.'s picture.

Jeremy steps up next to Reed. "What are we staring at?" he asks.

"Nothing," Reed answers.

At that moment the door to the girls' locker room opens, letting forth a burst of shrieking and girlie laughter. Karyn Aufiero emerges looking like she's just stepped off a runway instead of coming from forty-five minutes of non-stop volleyball. Reed blushes. Why does she always have to look so perfect?

"Hi, guys," she says. She stops next to Jeremy and

mimics the guys' stance. "Why are we looking at T. J.'s picture?"

She and Jeremy both look at Reed out of the corner of their eyes, but he says nothing. It's not like he can tell them what he was really thinking before they came out here. Not that he doesn't want to. For the first time since it happened, he has this urge to talk. To tell someone what he did. To see what they'd actually think about it.

"That was some game," Jeremy says slowly, referring to the semifinal game that T. J. had dominated—the game that had solidified him as the best quarterback in the league and had basically won him the Athlete of the Year award that Reed can't seem to look away from.

"Yeah, so I've heard," Reed says, stuffing his hands in the front pockets of his jeans.

"Right, you were sick that weekend, weren't you?" Jeremy asks, adjusting his backpack on his shoulder.

Reed scoffs and kicks the wall beneath the trophy case. "Yeah, right."

Karyn and Jeremy glance at each other, confused, and Reed feels the skin on his neck grow even hotter. He's already said more than he'd intended to. *Change the subject,* he wills himself. *Just look away.*

"Yeah! I remember that," Karyn says. She turns to face them and leans her left shoulder against the trophy case. "You were all psyched for that game and then suddenly, like, the day before, you got this weird, random stomach thing. You didn't even dress."

Reed tips his head forward, staring at the floor, but he can still feel Jeremy studying him. He can practically feel the guy's brain working the whole thing out in his head. Jeremy may not be an honors student, but he is definitely perceptive.

"It was pretty sudden," Jeremy says, crossing his arms over his chest. "What was that all about anyway, man?"

"I don't know . . . nerves?" Reed says, finally turning his back to his brother's face. He leans back against the trophy case and wonders when the bell is going to ring.

"Right, like you'd be nervous about riding the bench," Jeremy says. Reed glances at him and Jeremy turns about ten shades of red. "I didn't mean it like that," he says. "I mean I—"

"It's okay," Reed says. He cracks a sudden smile. "It's just ironic." And then he realizes he's going to do it. He's going to give away the secret. And he actually wants to. "It's ironic because I *was* nervous. Because Coach was going to have me start."

Reed watches as Karyn and Jeremy's faces both go slack. "Coach was going to—" Jeremy begins.

"Take T. J. out," Reed finishes. He shrugs his shoulders up so high, they almost touch his ears. "T. J. was slacking and that was an important game. For some reason, Coach thought I could handle it. I don't know."

But he does know. He remembers every single thing the coach had said to him. *If we go to the championship game, I'm not sure I'm comfortable starting T. J. At this point, I see the starting quarterback position as up for grabs. I'm giving you your chance, Reed. Show me what you can do. Show me what you're made of.*

And Reed had shown him all right. He hadn't shown up at all.

"Why didn't you play?" Karyn says, her voice a near croak as if her throat has gone completely dry.

Because I'm not supposed to be better than T. J. Not at football. Not at sports. It's the only thing he has.

"I don't even remember," Reed lies, turning to stare— no, *glare*—at his brother's picture again. "It worked out anyway, right?" he adds lightly. "T. J. kicked ass that game. Three touchdowns, 212 yards passing. It was insane."

"Yeah," Jeremy says, obviously still confused. "It was insane."

Reed looks over at the article the paper had run about the game. Certain words jump out at him. *Unstoppable . . . born to throw a football . . . Frasier really shines. . . .*

If Reed had stepped in, T. J. would have been devastated. His mother would have been devastated. She probably never would have forgiven Reed for taking away the one thing T. J. had. There was no way Reed could have done that to his brother. Not after everything T. J. had done for him. All those times he had stepped in to help him. All those times T. J. had taken the blame. All those times his brother had faced his fear so that Reed wouldn't have to.

That day in the coach's office, it had seemed like the most natural decision in the world. He couldn't turn Coach Fedorchak down. The coach wouldn't have *let* him turn him down. So he'd known at that moment that he would be playing sick on game day.

Reed sighs as more and more people start to pour out of the locker rooms. He glances at Jeremy and Karyn. Jeremy quickly looks away, but it takes Karyn a second longer. And there's something in her eyes . . . like she's trying to figure something out that's just beyond her reach. About him? T. J.? What? Finally she turns her gaze as well.

They probably both think I'm out of my mind, Reed thinks as they all start off down the hallway together. *Maybe I am.* He grips the shoulder strap on his backpack with both hands and clenches his jaw as he walks. He knows he could have played that game just as well as T. J. had. It could have been *his* face up there in the trophy case, preserved for all time as one of Falls High's greatest heroes.

So why wasn't it? Why did he always have to take a backseat to his brother?

* * *

"There's my dad," Peter tells Jane, lifting his chin in the direction of his father's car, which is parked along the curb in front of the school a few dozen yards from the door. Jane maneuvers their way over.

"Hi, Mr. Davis," Jane says as Peter's father lifts his long, lanky frame out of the driver's seat.

Mr. Davis looks at Jane just a moment too long before saying hello, making it abundantly clear that he has no idea who she is. *Real smooth,* Peter thinks, feeling his face heat up as Jane clears her throat and looks away.

"It's Jane, Dad," Peter says. "Remember? Jane Scott?"

"Oh yes, right," his father says stiffly. Peter knows his father is remembering now. Remembering why he knows Jane Scott's name so well. Remembering the way Jane cried and blubbered all over him on that day so many years ago. Peter's dad has never been comfortable with emotional outbursts. Or emotions of any kind, for that matter.

"Well, I guess I'd better go," Jane says, backing away. "I've got a lot to do."

She lifts her hand and turns on her heel. Peter watches her speed walk toward her car and wonders if she's having the same flashback he and his father are having. Even if she's not, he understands her hasty retreat. There isn't much of a comfort zone when Peter and his dad are together.

Peter's father walks around the front of the car and opens the passenger side door. He steps back as Peter wheels himself over to the car and looks down at the seat. It seems miles away. He would give anything to be able to get himself in there. To feel like he was capable of doing something as simple as transferring himself from one seat to another.

His father steps in front of his chair and grasps Peter's arms. Peter leans forward and clutches his father's elbows as his dad awkwardly pulls him out of the chair and deposits him in the car. The whole process takes seconds, but they are agonizing, humiliating seconds. His father bends to shift Peter's legs inside, but Peter holds out a hand to stop him.

"I got it!" he says, his face burning from exertion and humiliation. He and his father hadn't touched in years before the accident. Now that his survival basically depends on contact, it makes him feel like he's a toddler. Peter reaches down and lifts first his left leg, then his right into the car, resting his feet on the floor mat.

His father waits until he's safely inside, then slams the door and collapses the wheelchair, shoving it into the trunk. By the time he gets behind the wheel, Peter's breathing has finally returned to normal.

"So," his father says, clearing his throat. "I have the rest of the day off. Do you . . . want to go to the mall or something?"

There's no eye contact as this question is asked, but Peter's almost too surprised by the words to even notice. His father is actually suggesting they spend time together?

"Actually, I'd rather just go home," he says. "I have a lot of studying to do."

His father's head snaps to the right so fast, Peter's afraid it's going to snap right off. *Now* there's eye contact.

"I have a lot to catch up on," Peter says with a quick shrug as if he's always been Mr. Responsible Bookworm Boy. "I've gotten a couple of good grades and I feel like I'm sort of on a roll. Might as well ride it while it lasts."

There's a long silence and Peter starts to get annoyed. He's never been a good student, but he hadn't thought this news would be shocking enough to render his father mute *and* immobile.

"Dad?" Peter says finally, staring at his father's lifeless face.

"Sorry," Mr. Davis says, reaching up to start the car. "I'm just . . . wow. It's nice to hear you so excited about your work." He looks at Peter again, this time with an unfamiliar glint in his eye and a rare smile on his face. "Never thought I'd see the day," he says in a joking tone.

"Yeah, me neither," Peter says with a smile. He's having a conversation with his father. That's what this is, isn't it? An actual conversation?

His father puts his hands on the wheel, looks in the side mirror, then sighs. "I'm proud of you, son," he says, eyes trained on the windshield. "The way you're handling all this and . . . I'm just . . . I'm proud of you."

Peter's heart melts, warming his whole body. He feels like it's going to come spilling out through his pores even as he feels some tears threatening. He doesn't remember the last time his father told him he was proud of him. In fact, he's almost certain his father has *never* said that to him.

"Thanks, Dad," he says finally.

As his father pulls out of the parking lot and starts to pick up speed, Peter feels a sense of peace come over him. Everything's changing. Everything feels different. Better. Less . . . hard. How is that possible when he's in a wheelchair? Can it really be that he feels this way because of what his father just said to him? And if so, what can he do to get him to say it again? And again? As often as conceivably possible?

Peter sighs and smiles, looks down at his lifeless legs. One of these days, everything is going to be fine. He can feel it. And just imagine how proud his father's going to be the day he starts walking again.

CHAPTER SiX

Okay, when I'm *done with this, I'll do my calc problems, then my history chapter, then the reading for African-American lit. After dinner I'll practice for another hour, then work on the Web site, then deal with one of those applications. That means I'll have to—*

"Jane! I don't hear you practicing!"

Jane's arms tense up and she brings her sax to her lips so fast, she bangs her teeth with the mouthpiece.

"Dammit," she says under her breath, bringing her hand to her mouth. She looks down at the piece of music before her and the notes blur before her eyes, making the page look like a streaky mishmash of lines and notes. Jane couldn't play this if she tried. It's a complex piece and her brain is too overloaded to even begin.

But she knows her mother is standing at the bottom of the stairs, waiting to hear something, so she puts the reed between her lips and plays a B-flat scale. Up, then down. That oughta hold her off for about fifteen seconds.

Jane shakes back her hair and tries to concentrate on the music. She loves this piece. The band had played it when she was a freshman and everything was new and exciting and pure. Now Mr. Vega, the band director, is bringing it back and Jane should be psyched. She should be able to play the thing from memory.

But all she can remember is how happy music used to make her feel. How picking up her sax once brought her to a whole other place. How it used to relax her.

And how now, whenever she touches the thing, every muscle in her body tenses up—even her heart. Especially her heart.

"This is ridiculous," Jane says, flipping through the music to the next piece in the booklet. It's another good song, but not as difficult. Jane brings the sax to her lips again and plays a few notes. They squeak out violently like she's beating a bagpipe.

"Ugh!"

Jane stands up and starts to walk around her room, her sax hanging from its cord around her neck. She holds her forehead with one hand as if she's afraid her brain is going to explode out the front of her skull if she doesn't hold it in. And the way she's going lately, it just might.

I can't do this anymore, Jane's mind wails. *When I'm playing, I feel guilty because I should be studying. When I'm studying, I feel guilty because I should be playing. And all of it is pointless. All of it!*

She can sense her mother downstairs. Can picture her in

the kitchen—silent, motionless, listening. Getting more and more agitated with every moment that passes sans music.

She can't do this to me, Jane thinks, hot tears stinging at her eyes. *This used to be what I loved, but I can't even do it now. Why can't they both just leave me alone?*

Jane drops back down into the desk chair in front of her music stand. She wants so much to make both her parents happy. Can't stand the thought of disappointing them. So she has to keep working. Keep trying. But why? She's already disappointed them. She's already ripped all their dreams for her to shreds and they don't even know it yet.

I have to tell them. I can't take this anymore. I have to tell them. . . .

Jane tries to imagine where she'll be at this time next year. She tries to see a future that her parents will be happy with. But her mind, for once, is completely blank. All she sees is a fuzzy gray screen. Jane Scott is going nowhere.

"Janie?"

There's a light knock at the door. Jane sniffles, sits up straight, and wipes beneath her eyes with her hands. By the time she tells her mother to come in, she's the picture of composure, sax at the ready, reed just millimeters from her lips.

"Everything okay?" her mother asks, looking around as she enters the room. "I haven't heard much out of you today."

"I've just been going over the music," Jane says automatically. "You know, I like to do that before I play—kind of absorb it first."

It's a total lie, but at least it makes her mother's eyes shine with pride. Like her daughter is just *so* in tune with her craft.

"Well, I wanted to let you know that I've agreed to let your father take you to Boston this weekend," she says, sitting down gingerly on the edge of Jane's bed.

Jane feels her heart sink into her toes. She'd really been hoping her mother would win that particular argument. Going to Boston is just going to make her father salivate over the schools there even more. It's just going to make Jane more miserable and guilty. Why is she letting it go this far? Maybe the kinder thing would be to just tell her parents. Let them stop hoping. Stop dreaming.

There's a prolonged silence and Jane suddenly realizes she's expected to speak.

"Oh," she says glancing at her mother. "Great."

"There is a condition, though," her mom continues.

What? That I play the saxophone twenty-four hours a day while I'm there? She pictures herself taking a tour of Harvard with a posse of stuffed shirts, playing "Louie Louie" on her sax the whole way.

"He's going to take you to Boston Conservatory as well," Jane's mother finishes, a bright smile on her face. She looks at Jane expectantly, waiting for her to jump up with glee, no doubt. Unfortunately the heaviness in her chest prevents jumping of any kind.

"Oh," she says again, the near smile now gone. "Great."

"I'm sure they'll want to meet with you while you're there," her mother continues, oblivious. "After all, they've had your audition tape for a while. You should call to set up an interview."

Jane feels herself slowly being crushed. There is no audition tape. She's never sent one. Never even recorded one. Mr. Vega had told her it would be good to have an original piece, so Jane had asked Danny Chaiken to write one. But he'd kept putting her off. And Jane knows he'll probably never do it. From what she's heard, Danny was in a car accident and got suspended from school. He hasn't even been in class for the last two days.

But none of that matters to her mother. Especially not since Jane had told her she'd sent a tape in back in September.

"So, Jane, you'll call them, right?" her mother asks, placing her hands on her knees before she stands. "You should do it today or all the interview spots are going to fill up."

Jane blinks and looks up at her mother. "Yeah," she says flatly. "I'll call them."

"When?" her mother prompts, crossing her slim arms over her chest.

"Today," Jane responds.

"That's my girl."

Jane doesn't move an inch as her mother leaves the room, closing the door behind her. She knows she should get up and find the number for the conservatory. But she should also get up and find a piece to play for a tape she hasn't made. She should also get up and find a tape on which to record the piece she hasn't found. She should also get up and fill out the application to send with the tape of the piece she hasn't found.

And since each of these thoughts makes the crushing weight upon her that much heavier, Jane doesn't move at all.

• • •

Meena sits at the end of the leather couch in Dr. Lansky's waiting room, her knees pulled up under her chin, her arms wrapped tightly around her shins. She stares straight ahead at the framed poster across from her. Whenever she's here, she sits, waits, stares, and wishes she were anywhere but in this office.

"Meena?" Dr. Lansky calls out, opening the door to his office. Meena practically jumps out of her seat, grateful for an interruption of the dialogue in her head. If this keeps up, they're going to be fitting her for a straitjacket before she knows it.

Turning sideways to get through the door, Meena slips past Dr. Lansky and sits down in the middle of the couch across from his chair. She places her feet on the floor and folds her hands in her lap. Today she has decided to look the picture of mental health. Maybe if she can convince Lansky that everything is fine, she won't have to come here anymore.

But if you're not going to come here, where will you go? her mind asks. *At least on shrink days you don't have to deal with being at home.*

Meena takes a deep breath and tries to shut out the voice. Hanging out at the diner or even on the street would be better than getting analyzed by Lansky. She can't stand the condescending, probing look in his eyes. She knows he *thinks* he's coming off as kind, but she can't stand the way he looks at her. Like he knows something, knows what she's hiding.

"So, how's our little experiment going?" Dr. Lansky asks as he settles into his chair with his pad in front of him. He reaches up and scratches an itch beneath his gray beard.

"Okay," Meena says. She has to concentrate to keep from squirming.

Dr. Lansky smiles a little half smile, more like a smirk. "Care to elaborate on that?"

No. Meena squeezes her hands together more tightly and tells herself to chill and answer the question.

"I've been eating more . . . ," she says, looking down at her lap. "Getting up on time like you said. . . ." Meena glances up at him to see if she's said enough, but it's clear from his raised eyebrows that he's expecting more.

"And how is school?" he asks.

She shrugs and slumps. "Fine . . . better . . . I guess," she says as her eyes dart to the window and back down to her hands again. "It's been easier to pay attention lately."

There. That sounded good.

"Why is that, do you think?" Lansky asks, shifting his legs to cross one over the other.

Why are you asking me *that?* Meena's mind shouts. *You're the shrink!*

"I don't know," she says. She glances at her watch. Less than four minutes have passed. She's never going to get out of here.

"Okay, tell me about home," Lansky says, ever patient.

Home. Well, I'm afraid to set foot through the door. I'm barely sleeping because I'm always scared, and my parents think I'm a nutcase. Other than that, home is—

"Fine," she blurts out. Then a hot blush covers her face because she knows she's not making any sense.

"Home is fine?" he asks.

"Yep."

"And how are you sleeping?"

"Well, if it weren't for the nightmares—"

Meena's whole body goes rigid as sweat pops out along her hairline. Her eyes dart to Lansky and he's already writing it down. She can't believe she just said that. How could she have let that out? He's definitely going to ask her to *elaborate* on that one.

You should never have started talking in the first place, the little voice in her mind tells her. *You're so stupid, Meena. Why can't you just keep your mouth shut?*

"You've been having nightmares?" Lansky asks. His stance remains calm—one arm on the armrest with his hand to his chin, the other hand holding the pen poised. But Meena can tell he's psyched. She knows what he's thinking—*What a breakthrough! The girl is insane! How good am I?*

Meena pushes her sweaty palms into the thighs of her jeans, rubbing them repeatedly. "No. I mean, not really. I don't know why I said that." She adds a little laugh for effect, but Lansky doesn't back down.

"It's okay, Meena," Dr. Lansky says. "This is good. It's good to talk about these things. Now, are you having them every night?"

Yes. "I wouldn't say *every* night. . . ."

Lansky makes a note. Glances over the page quickly. "What are they about?" he asks.

They're about what happened to me when I was ten. They're about what's happening to me now. They're all mixed up and they don't make any sense. They're awful and vivid and I always think I'm going to die.

"I don't remember," Meena lies.

"So you just wake up knowing you've had a nightmare?" Lansky prods.

Meena's legs draw up under her chin again. "I guess." She doesn't want to talk about this. Can't he tell she doesn't want to talk about this? Or does he just not care?

You're the one who brought it up, stupid, her mind shouts. *You should have known better. Now you're never going to get out of therapy.*

Dr. Lansky takes a long, deep breath and lets it out slowly, scribbling down something else on his pad. Meena glances up and glares at his pen as it flies across the page. What is he writing about her? And why does he have to take notes anyway? So that he doesn't forget the details when he reports back to her parents about what a wack job she is?

"Okay, Meena," Dr. Lansky says, laying down his pen and looking at her. "I understand if you don't want to talk about your dreams. They're very private things. But why don't you try keeping a dream journal?"

Meena snorts a laugh. Like she really wants to record those awful nightmares for posterity.

"It can be really good for you," Dr. Lansky explains in his standard condescending tone. "It might help you get to the root of your problem."

Meena looks at him—dead in the eye—for the first time all day. And she realizes he's actually serious. He actually expects her to wake up, heart pounding, hair sticking to her face, and write down what she's just dreamed. She's not the only nut job in this room.

"Will you do that?" Dr. Lansky says. "You don't have to show it to me if you don't want to."

Meena rolls her eyes and looks down again. "Fine."

"And keep up with the eating and the getting up on time and the rest of it, okay?" Dr. Lansky says, making a couple more notes.

"Fine," Meena repeats almost under her breath.

All you had to do was stay quiet, but apparently you can't even do that, she thinks, tears clouding her vision. *You can't do anything right.*

• • •

"I told you it would be worth the effort," Cori says, crooking her arm behind her head and lying back on the blanket she'd spread across the ground.

Danny turns his head to look at her, just inches away, and even though the ground is hard and he's freezing his butt off, he has to agree. Anything would be worth lying here on the ninth green with Cori. Of course, it's not like he'd ever say it.

"I did enjoy the whole fence-scaling thing," he tells her. "But you owe me a pair of jeans."

"I mentioned that there might be casualties," Cori says with a smirk. "You were warned."

Danny laughs and returns his attention to the sky. After much debate over whether or not Danny should be allowed to go out, followed by even more debate over whether or not he should be allowed to drive his car, his parents had consented to let him go to Cori's to study. His mom had dropped him off at Cori's house but decided it was okay to let Cori drive him home. After a successful study session that was about sixty percent studying, ten percent snacking, and thirty percent laughing, Cori had suggested they make a pit stop on the way home. Danny, who had felt blissfully even all night long, had been nothing but psyched at the suggestion.

So a few minutes ago he and Cori had jumped the chain-link fence that surrounds the golf course at the Winetka Falls Country Club. Danny, of course, had snagged the pocket of his favorite jeans on his way down. The snag had resulted in a comical and bruising fall, but Danny doesn't mind any of it. The only thing he minds is that now that he's here, the fog is starting to return. The fog in his mind that makes everything numb. The medication is kicking in and it couldn't have picked a worse moment to make itself known.

Fight it, Danny tells himself. *You have to feel every minute of this.*

He takes a deep breath and focuses. Cori is inches away. It's dark. There are stars. Loads of 'em.

"I gotta admit, this is pretty amazing," Danny says, folding his hands on his stomach and tilting his head a bit closer to Cori's. He feels her hair brush his cheek and it sends a shiver down his whole left side. Danny smiles. He's not *totally* numb . . . yet.

"I knew you would like it," Cori says. "It's a perfect night for it."

"Yeah," Danny says. It sounds detached and he feels himself start to float with the fog. He blinks a few times, trying to clear his mind and bring himself back, but it doesn't help much.

You can't control it, he reminds himself, trying not to get upset. *At least you're not manic. If you were hyper and edgy right now, that'd be a lot worse.*

"My brother, Chris, used to come out here all the time with his friends," Cori tells Danny. He closes his eyes as she tells the story, bobbing through the ether with her words. "On nights when he was stuck baby-sitting me, he'd bring me along.

They'd just sit out here and drink and look at the stars. . . ."

"Sounds nice," Danny says with a smile.

"Right! He was a total delinquent!" Cori says, nudging Danny with her shoulder. He blinks, startled, and wonders what he said wrong. But he can't even remember what he said.

Focus, he tells himself. *You can't blow this now.*

"So anyway, I hated the smell of the vodka and stuff, so I'd sit over there by the fence and name the stars," Cori says.

"Really?" Danny forces his eyebrows up. It takes a lot of effort in his foggy state. "What did you name them?"

"Oh . . . let's see," Cori says, hoisting herself up onto her elbows. "There's Gumdrop . . . Care Bear. . . ." She points to a few stars, a totally serious look on her face, as if she were a professional astronomer and these were actual, scientific names. "There were two that were close to each other named Barbie and Ken."

Danny turns onto his side. "You are a monster dork," he says with a grin, leaning his head on his hand.

"That's *such* an insult coming from a guy who still wears Simpsons T-shirts," Cori jokes back.

"Hey! The Simpsons are the most important cultural contribution of the late twentieth century," Danny tells her, feigning offense. "Except for *Star Wars.*"

They both laugh and Danny realizes that the fog is not totally unpleasant. It makes her laughter stay with him and circle around him like a warm blanket.

Just as he's pondering this feeling, he notices that Cori

seems to be getting a lot closer. His heart lurches when he realizes her eyes are closing. She's leaning in to kiss him!

That's nice, he thinks through his fog. *Cori is going to kiss me.*

Don't! a sudden, panicked voice shouts from the back of his mind. *Don't let her! Stop her!*

Before Danny can comprehend what he's doing, he pulls back. "We should really go."

Cori flips onto her back abruptly and clears her throat, obviously flustered.

Oh God! What did I just do? Why didn't I just let her kiss me? I've only been dreaming about it for months! But I can't. I can't get involved with her. I can't let her know what a freak I am.

Cori deserves better than him. So very much better. She deserves somebody normal. Somebody who doesn't deck teachers, who doesn't get depressed for no reason, who doesn't need to pop pills twice a day just to appear sane.

"I'm sorry," Danny says, sitting up. "It's just . . . you know . . . my parents. They're gonna kill me if I'm, like, five seconds late."

"Iknowl'msorryIdon'twanttogetyouintrouble." Cori's words are a blur as she stands up.

Danny has to scoot off the blanket as she gathers it up in a ball in her arms. He gazes up at her as she clutches the wool to her body, his pulse pounding. She's never going to speak to him again.

Then she takes a deep breath, blows it out in a cloud of mist, and smiles. "So let's go," she says.

Danny blinks. He can't believe it. She's actually being cool about this? Not flustered and mortified and angry? He gets up slowly and whacks at the backs of his legs to clear the dirt from his ripped jeans.

Maybe she wasn't trying to kiss me, Danny thinks foggily. *Maybe I just imagined it.*

Unfortunately, as he follows Cori across the golf course, he's not sure whether he should be comforted or depressed by this thought.

• • •

"You can't catch me, Jane! You can't catch me!"

Jane chases Meena Miller around and around and around an old, fraying couch, watching Meena's long hair bounce and swing around. She laughs as she reaches out to grab her friend, but Meena pulls away just in time.

"You give?" Meena says, stopping and gasping for breath.

It's only now that Jane realizes that Meena is a little girl. But she's looking Meena right in the eye, so Jane must be a little girl, too.

"Let's play something else," Meena says with a shrug. Then she takes off again, walking across the room. She looks under a chair, then lifts up a beanbag to look under that. She peeks into a cabinet.

"What are you looking for?" Jane asks, following slowly behind. Her heart is starting to pound. She doesn't like this game.

"You know what I'm looking for," Meena says. She turns to Jane and she's smiling, but something in her eyes is off.

"I don't want to play this," Jane whines, wringing her hands.

"Oh yes, you do," Meena says. She walks over to a closet, and the closer Meena gets, the more frightened Jane becomes. There's something in there. Something scary. Something she doesn't want to see.

Meena's little hand reaches for the doorknob and Jane lets out a scream. "Nooooo!"

But Meena opens the door and nothing happens. She turns to look at Jane and grins. "Come on."

Still shaking, Jane walks over to the closet and peeks inside. But there's nothing scary in there. Nothing but boxes with labels written in red marker. They say things like Pictures, Kitchen, College. Meena sits down and pulls a box off a shelf. She pulls up the flaps and lifts out a piece of paper.

Jane looks over her shoulder. It's a chemistry test done in her handwriting and there's a big red F marked on the front page. Jane's breath catches and she tries to snatch the page away, but Meena holds it out of her reach.

"You got an F?" Meena screeches, her eyes wide. She laughs and looks down into the box, pulling out page after page. "These are all Fs!" she says gleefully. "You're a failure, Jane! A failure and a fake!"

"Stop it, Meena! Stop it!" Jane shouts, starting to cry. But Meena doesn't listen. She keeps pulling page after page out of the box, letting them drift to the floor and out the door. Jane tries to gather them up and stuff them in her pockets, but there are just

111

too many. Everywhere she looks, all she sees is F . . . F . . . F . . . F . . . F.

Then Meena finally stops unearthing papers and pulls down a little box from the highest shelf. Jane's heart stops the instant she sees it.

"Don't open that," she tells Meena. "We'll get in trouble." She reaches for the box, but Meena pulls it away, laughing at her.

"What do you know, failure?" she says with a smirk.

"Meena, don't!" Jane screams. "Don't do that! DON'T!"

Still laughing, Meena lifts the lid and everything explodes.

Jane's eyes pop open. Her heart is racing as she sits up and looks around her darkened bedroom, struggling to recall the dream.

"What do you know, failure?"

"Oh God!" Jane whispers. She flings her covers aside and hits the floor on her knees. Then she lifts her mattress and sticks her hand between it and the box spring, searching blindly.

"Where is it, where is it, where is it?" she repeats under her breath as she searches back and forth. It's not there. Oh God. It's not there. Her mother must have found it. But how? And when? Jane was in here studying all night. How could she have—

And then, just as she's about to burst into hysterical tears, her fingers touch paper and Jane pulls out the tattered, flattened sheet. The scores are still there. She's safe . . . for now.

CHAPTER SEVEN

When the bell rings to end music theory class on Wednesday afternoon, Jane is the first person out of her seat. The moment she sees Danny Chaiken trying to make a fast escape, she bolts across the room in three long strides. He glimpses her coming and tries to slip out, but she's too fast.

"Danny," she says, reaching out to grab his arm. He looks down at her hand and she flinches, pulling it away. After all, he *did* deck a teacher last week, so he might not be the best person to provoke. "Did you write it?" she asks. "Tell me you wrote it."

She knows she's grasping at straws, but she has no idea what she's going to play on her audition tape. And maybe Danny *did* do it, even after she stalked away from him last week. Maybe he had so much time on his hands during his suspension . . .

Danny's chin drops forward and he pulls the pen he's been chewing on all period out of his mouth. "I didn't write it," he says, his voice full of remorse. Jane feels her heart drop down through the rubber soles of her sneakers. "I'm sorry, Jane."

If she doesn't get a tape in right away, she's not going to be able to set up an interview for this weekend. And if she doesn't set up an interview, her mother is going to want to know why. And she can't tell her mother why. It's the reason she's still putting herself through all of this, even knowing that it's pointless—to avoid having to say those words to her mother.

"I'm sorry," Danny says again. And to his credit, he really does look upset. "I wanted to help you, but I've . . . I've just had a lot going on lately."

Jane takes another long, calming breath and lets it out slowly and audibly. "It's okay," she says, listening to the rapid beating of her pulse. She glances at Mr. Vega, who's packing up his briefcase at the front of the room.

"Don't worry about it. I'll see you later," she tells Danny, waving him off as she turns and makes a beeline for the teacher. He's the only one who can help her now.

"Mr. Vega!" she says, stepping in front of him as he heads for the door. She clutches her notebook and planner to her chest as if she's holding on for dear life. "Can I ask a favor?"

Just say yes, she begs silently. *I have to get this over with.*

"Sure, Jane," the teacher says, putting his free hand in the pocket of his gray slacks. He smiles his friendly smile and Jane calms down just slightly.

"I need to make a tape for Boston Conservatory," she says, biting her bottom lip. "This afternoon."

Mr. Vega's bushy eyebrows shoot up. "I don't know. Do you have a piece prepared?"

"Of course!" she lies, clueless as to whether she's even going to be able to *play* this afternoon. She's barely gotten in any decent rehearsal time all week. "I really have to get the tape out ASAP." *Like three months ago.*

"Okay . . . let's see. . . ." Mr. Vega steps over to his desk and flips a few pages on his daily calendar. "Well, it looks like I'm free. I'll meet you in the studio after school."

"Thanks," Jane says, not even registering relief. If anything, the tension just builds up more. She turns around, her mind already racing ahead to the next task. It's not like she can just *decide* to do something after school. This little change of schedule is going to throw everything else out of whack.

Jane takes off into the crowded hallway, her eyes scanning the faces all around her. She has to find Reed before he gets to his next class. Because if she's going to make the tape this afternoon, that means she's going to have to go right to FedEx and send it out, which means not only will she miss Academic Decathlon practice, but she won't make her shift at TCBY, either.

Dodging and weaving her way toward the main hall, Jane racks her brain, trying to figure out if she knows what class Reed has next. It's the middle of the day, which means it could be lunch or gym. Luckily both the cafeteria and the gymnasium are off the main hall, so she has a good chance of catching him.

As she rounds the corner, she catches a glimpse of three guys in varsity jackets striding down the hall away from her. One of them is wearing Reed's signature baseball cap.

"Reed!" she shouts.

He turns and scans the hallway. Jane lifts her hand and Reed says something to his friends, then waits for her to catch up. By the time she does, she's out of breath.

"You all right?" Reed asks, concern creasing his face.

"Fine," Jane says. Now that she's stopped, she can feel the heat of exertion prickling all over her skin. She has to calm down. But she can't. She has too much to take care of. "Listen, I have something I have to do today. Is there any way you can take my shift?"

"Again?" Reed says, his blue eyes widening. He looks off down the hall as he thinks it over. "Yeah, I guess," he says.

Jane's about to thank him and run off, glad that at least one thing has gotten done, when he stops her. "If you take my shift tomorrow," he adds.

Her back goes rigid and her grip on her notebook tightens, the little coiled wire digging into her fingers. Slowly she opens her planner. Aside from all the assignments she's written down for tomorrow, she also has an Academic Decathlon meet right after school and practice for her volunteer orchestra tomorrow night. But she can miss that. They don't have any big charity performances coming up. She'll just tell them she's sick. All of the other orchestra members go to other schools, so none of them will know she's lying. Besides, she's never missed it before.

Of course, Mom will kill you, but that's another story.

"Fine," she says, the word clipped with tension. "I can do that."

"Cool," Reed says.

Jane can tell he's about to ask her something else, but she turns and heads down the stairs to the lobby before he can get it out. She's pretty sure she hears him call after her, "Hey! Did you get your scores?" but she chooses to ignore him.

Scurrying across the lobby, Jane flips through her planner to the phone book in the back. She slides to a stop in front of the pay phone and quickly dials in her calling card number. If she doesn't call the volunteer orchestra now, she won't have time later.

Speaking of time . . . Jane glances at her watch. The bell is going to ring any minute. She is just reaching up a shaky finger to dial in the number of the orchestra's secretary when the planner slips out of her hand and hits the floor. The binder pops open and pages go flying everywhere . . . just as the bell rings.

"Dammit!" Jane mutters.

She drops to the floor, letting the phone dangle, and gathers up the pages. They're all out of order, but she doesn't have time to deal with them now. On the verge of tears, Jane gathers up the pages in her arms, rumpling and crinkling them beyond repair, and runs off for class, the phone beeping in protest behind her.

• • •

Don't look at it. Just don't even look, Reed tells himself as he walks past the trophy case heading for gym class on Wednesday afternoon. His hands are clenched and in the mood he's in right now, there's a good chance he'll put his fist through the glass if he even glances at his brother's smiling portrait.

What is wrong with me? he wonders, trying to uncoil his fingers. *Why do I let T. J. walk all over me? I do his chores, I pick up his clothes, I let him say whatever he wants to me . . . about me. And why? Seriously . . . why? Just because he has a disability?*

Reed turns the corner and leans back against the cool cinder block wall, slowly breathing in and out. This mind-racing thing is a new sensation for him. Normally he's totally levelheaded and rational, so the random floods of thoughts he's been having ever since Jeremy brought up the oddities of his relationship with T. J. the other day are new to him.

New and annoying. Reed doesn't like feeling out of control. He doesn't like feeling like a basket case.

But it's not just because of his dyslexia, you know that, his brains chides him. *He protected you. He was always there. . . .*

Reed pulls off his baseball cap, runs his hand through his hair, then pulls the cap back on tightly. He squeezes his eyes shut, trying to push the images that are starting to seep into his mind right back out. He doesn't want to remember. He's spent most of his life trying to forget.

Of course T. J. protected me, he thinks. *He's the older brother. It's his job. If I'd been the older brother, I would have protected him. But no. T. J. is older. And because of that he's on the football team at*

Boston College and I have no chance of getting a scholarship because I never started a game until this year . . . thanks to him.

"He gets to have everything," Reed mutters under his breath, his fists clenching again as Karyn's smiling face drifts through his mind. "Everything."

At that moment, as if she knows he's thinking of her, Karyn walks around the corner and her whole face lights up the second she sees Reed. It makes him both elated and sick.

"There you are!" she says, tossing her long blond hair behind her shoulder. She's wearing a tightish red sweater that brings out the color in her face, and as she walks over to him and circles his arm with her own, her perfume fills his senses. It's all Reed can do to keep from going weak in the knees. The girl even *smells* perfect.

"I was hoping I'd catch you before you hit the locker room," Karyn says. "Please tell me we're still on for a calc session tonight. I am *so* lost."

Reed's jaw clenches and he steps back abruptly. "I can't," he says.

But he means more than the calc study session. He can't do any of this anymore. He can't go around pretending he's just her friend. He can't look at her, touch her, *smell* her when he knows that T. J. gets to do so much more. It's not fair.

"What's wrong?" Karyn asks, her expression a mixture of disappointment and concern.

"I have to work," he tells her. At least it's not a lie, thanks to Jane.

"Oh," she says, hugging her notebooks to her chest. "Reed, are you okay?"

"I'm fine!" he spits out. Then he feels his face flush. "I just . . . I have to go."

"Reed . . ."

"I need to be alone, all right?" he blurts. Then he turns and stalks into the locker room. As soon as the door swings shut behind him, he feels like a complete moron. Why did he yell at Karyn? It's not like *she's* done anything. But he can't help it. He just can't be around her right now.

●●●

"Okay, everyone, we're going to go over the pre– and post–World War II geography of Europe one more time," Mr. Boyle says, earning a few groans from the back of the classroom. The teacher turns and glares right at Danny.

I didn't make a sound! Danny wants to shout. And normally he probably would, just to get a few laughs. But today he just sinks farther down in his chair. A few people around him shift in their seats uncomfortably. It's like they're all waiting for him to explode.

Do you blame them? Danny asks himself, gazing down at the top of his desk. *They're probably all wigged out that you're even back in school.*

It isn't fair. He did one thing wrong and now everyone expects it of him. And he feels fine today. Conspicuous, but otherwise fine. There aren't going to be any gossipworthy events courtesy of Danny this afternoon. He feels like he should walk around with a sign hanging from his neck, letting everyone know what to expect from him—Manic Day, Sleepy Day, Normal Day.

Cori clears her throat and Danny glances over at her. She's sitting just to his right and she holds up a piece of folded paper, then smiles and drops it on the floor between their desks. It makes an impossibly loud slapping sound.

Danny's heart hits his throat and his eyes dart to the front of the room. Luckily Boyle's attention is on the map as Cori uses the toe of her boot to shove the note closer to Danny, scraping it against the dirty floor. Watching the teacher's every move, Danny quickly leans down and snatches up the paper. Normally he wouldn't care about getting caught reading a note in class, but things are no longer normal.

As he unfolds the note, he's hovering somewhere between being angry at Cori for risking getting him in trouble and being totally psyched she's written him a note.

The paper seems to make enough noise to wake the dead as he flattens it on his desk, but no one else seems to notice. Danny grins when he reads it: *Free tomorrow tonight? I found a place you'll love.*

He feels a scorching blush take over his cheeks and takes a deep breath, willing it away. But he can't ignore the back flips his heart is doing. She wants to see him again. The aborted kiss didn't kill their friendship. And maybe it'll happen again. Maybe *he'll* kiss *her*. Finally. After all this time.

God. Him and Cori. That would be so—

Not possible, the little voice in Danny's mind cuts in. *You can't be with her. She doesn't know what a psycho you are.*

Danny's fingers curl into fists. There's no way he can risk letting Cori know the real him. As much as the idea kills him inside, Danny is going to have to nip this thing in the bud.

He looks at her apologetically as he lifts his pen to respond, but Cori immediately turns her hand over and uses her pen to write something across it in big block letters. Danny watches her, confused, until she lifts her hand and arches her eyebrows hopefully. The note reads *PLEASE!*

Danny's whole body tingles and a grin involuntarily lights his face. It's unreal, the effect she has on him. He can already feel his determination starting to wane. It's not like he has manic episodes *all the time.* Chances are, Cori will never be around for a bad one. *At least, not again,* he thinks, glancing at Boyle.

Cori clears her throat and Danny looks at her, melting at the sight of her overexaggerated pout.

I have no choice here, he tells himself with an under-the-breath chuckle. *I am at this girl's mercy.*

He writes two letters on front of his notebook, then lifts his arm away so that she can see.

OK.

• • •

When the final bell of the day rings, Jane tears out into the hallway, heading for Ms. Motti's classroom. She knows that as soon as the halls fill up, she'll lose precious time, and she manages to get there before most of the kids have left their rooms. Ms. Motti is organizing some papers on her desk when Jane squeezes by a couple of outgoing students.

"Ms. Motti," she says, wiping the sleeve of her sweater across her brow and trying to catch her breath inconspicuously.

"Jane, what's the matter?" Ms. Motti asks. Her face, as always, is stern and she doesn't sound at all concerned. A lot of the things Ms. Motti says often sound preprogrammed.

"Nothing. I just ran here, basically," Jane says. Her heart is thumping, and not from the run. Ms. Motti is the least understanding teacher Jane has ever known. If she doesn't give Jane a hard time about what she's going to tell her, it'll be a miracle.

"Listen, I can't make practice this afternoon," Jane says, gripping her right hand with her left.

A flash of anger passes through Ms. Motti's plain brown eyes and her expression hardens. "I hope this is a joke," she says. "But I must tell you, it's not a very funny one, Ms. Scott."

Jane feels her stomach turn as she inches forward. All she wants is for one thing to work out today. Just one person to not give her a hard time or ask her to do more work. Can't anyone tell she's losing it here?

"Ms. Motti, I know tomorrow's meet is important—"

"The most important of the year," Ms. Motti says, putting her hands on her hips. "Randall High hasn't beat us in years. We have to keep the streak alive."

"I know that," Jane says, her throat dry. "But I have to make an audition tape this afternoon. It's really important to my—"

"You want to miss practice for a music activity?" Ms. Motti's voice is incredulous and Jane knows she's made a misstep. Ms. Motti could never understand how important her music is to her.

Or was . . . once, Jane thinks. Part of her wishes she could blow off the tape and come to Academic Decathlon practice. And another part of her wishes she could blow them both off. Just go somewhere and curl up in a ball and think about nothing for five minutes.

"I'm sorry," Jane says, trying to sound firm. "But I have to do this today. I'll get the material from Sumit tonight and I'll be prepared for the meet tomorrow."

Ms. Motti's nostrils actually flare and she looks down at her desk again, violently shuffling papers. "I'm very disappointed, Jane," she says to her desktop.

Jane stares at the top of Ms. Motti's head, covered with unkempt curls. She's not sure what she's supposed to do here. Is Ms. Motti letting her go? And even if she's not, what else can Jane say? She has to get to the studio right now or Mr. Vega's going to think she bailed. Jane hesitates a moment longer, opens her mouth, shuts it again. Then she takes a step back, but it doesn't feel right to leave the room without permission.

"So . . . can I go?" she asks, irrationally hoping that the woman will smile sympathetically and give her consent.

"I can't stop you," Ms. Motti says testily, without looking up.

Near tears, Jane turns and stalks out of the room. Why is it that every one of her teachers and advisers thinks their class or project is the only thing she has to do? Can't anyone cut her just the most minute bit of slack?

By the time she gets to Mr. Vega's room and opens the door to the studio attached, Jane's eyes are filled to the brim. There's a music stand in the center of the small room with a chair in front of it and Mr. Vega is already sitting at the mixing board with his headphones on. He looks up with his usual wide grin the moment Jane arrives, but it quickly fades.

"Are you okay?" he asks her.

Jane instantly blinks back her tears. "I'm fine," she says, dropping her backpack and sax case onto the floor. She yanks open the zipper on her bag and whips out the piece of music she decided to play at some point that afternoon— somewhere between falling on her face in gym and messing up the problem on the board in AP calculus. Then she takes out her saxophone and drops into the hard chair, slapping the pages of music onto the stand.

"Let's just do this," she says, bringing the mouthpiece to her lips. She does a quick scale to warm up, but she's shaking so much she falters twice. That never happens. Ever. Mr. Vega looks horrified.

"Take a few deep breaths," he suggests in his warm, calming voice.

"I just want to get this over with," she says, her fingers hovering over the keys on the sax. "Are you recording?"

"Okay," Mr. Vega says skeptically. "If you think you're ready. Just wait for my cue."

He turns in his chair and adjusts a few things, hits a few buttons. Jane holds her breath the whole time, telling herself to calm down. She's picked a piece she knows she can play. She just has to get this over with and get it sent out and then her mother will never know that she didn't do it months ago.

Mr. Vega turns a knob and the little green light on the wall goes on. He points at Jane and she finally exhales, then starts to play.

Badly.

Three stanzas in, Mr. Vega hits the pause button and takes off his headphones. Jane's whole back is taut with tension. Mr. Vega cuts right to the chase.

"Are you sure you want to do this today?" he asks, raising his eyebrows. "Maybe you should go home and rest and we'll try it tomorrow."

"No," Jane says flatly. "It has to be today. I'll be fine."

"Okay," Mr. Vega says. He looks Jane right in the eye and she stares back steadily. "But remember, Jane, this is very important."

Jane's eyes narrow and she feels her whole face crumple into a scowl. "I know it is," she says. *And so is my AD meet, and so is my job, and so is my homework, and the paper, and my tons of applications. It's all important. I get it.*

Lifting her instrument to her lips again, she waits for Mr. Vega's cue and starts to play. If she can just get through this piece, then something will be done. And once something's done, she can move on to the next thing. And the next. And the next . . .

CHAPTER EIGHT

"**Okay, just walk** in and go right upstairs," Jane whispers to herself as she approaches her front door on Wednesday evening.

She's exhausted from over an hour of playing and recording, then rushing across town to FedEx her tape to Boston Conservatory. But even though she feels like she could fall asleep while walking, Jane's whole body is on high alert. She knows her mom is going to want to talk to her the moment she walks through the door. Ask her about her scores, her schoolwork, her band practice.

But all Jane wants is five minutes of peace. Five minutes to attempt to breathe.

She opens the front door very quietly, steps inside, and shuts it behind her. She makes it all the way to the foot of the stairs before her mother catches her.

"Jane?" she says, walking into the foyer from the kitchen, her arms crossed over her chest. "Your father's on the phone. He'd like to speak to you."

Jane tries not to make the collapse of her body obvious. She places her bags down at the bottom of the steps and follows her mother into the kitchen without saying a word. So much for peace.

The phone is lying on the counter and Jane picks it up, stifling a yawn even through her heightened tension. "Hi, Dad," she says.

"Hello, Janie," he returns brightly. "I was just calling to see if you're all ready for the big meet tomorrow."

Jane looks down at the floor, kicking her sneaker against the tiles. She wonders if either of her parents has ever simply asked her how she is. It's always, *Are you ready? Did you do this? How well do you think you did on that? When are you going to—*

"Of course," she says, even though she skipped practice and has no idea what subject she's been assigned to cover. "Aren't I always prepared?" She means for that last bit to come out lighthearted, but it sounds more like a snap. Her mother frowns at her from across the kitchen.

"There's no reason to get snippy, Jane," her father says sternly.

"I know, Dad. I didn't mean it that way," Jane says quickly.

"Okay, then," he says. "So, did you get your scores yet?"

"No," Jane replies, squeezing her eyes shut. *Tell him. Just tell him. Just end it already.*

"Really? That's odd," he says.

"Is it?" Jane says weakly.

"Don't you think it's strange that everyone else in the area has gotten their scores, but you haven't?" he asks.

Just tell him. Just end it.

"It *is* weird," she says quickly. "Maybe I'll call the SAT people tomorrow and see what's up." She pushes herself away from the counter she's been leaning against and turns, ready to hang up the phone as soon as possible.

"Good idea," her father says, appeased.

"Dad, I have to go," she says. If she doesn't hang up soon, she's going to explode. "I'll talk to you later, okay?"

"Okay. Good luck tomorrow. Let me know how it goes," her father says.

"I will. Bye."

Jane hangs up the phone and quickly retreats from the room before her mother can question her further about her scores. She grabs her things and is halfway to her room when her mom calls up after her.

"Jane!"

She freezes. Rolls her eyes shut. Holds her breath. *Leave me alone!* her mind screams. *Just leave me alone for* five seconds!

"What?" she calls back, trying not to shout.

"Dinner's almost ready."

"I'll be down in a minute!" Jane says, her tears welling up again.

She storms into her room, throws her stuff down on her bed, and is about to lie down when she feels her computer pulling her toward her desk. As much as she wants to relax, she knows she won't feel comfortable resting until she checks for Sumit's e-mail about her topic for the debate.

Her back aching, Jane clicks into her e-mail and finds, among other things, a new message from Sumit titled "Big meet." She clicks it open and scans it. She's been assigned to history. *"Don't screw it up,"* Sumit writes. *"Randall High kicks at history and if we don't win, Ms. Motti is going to feed us to her dogs. I hear they're big. And smelly."*

Groaning, Jane closes the e-mail and drops into her chair. She rests her head on her hand and gazes over at her bookcases, which are packed with history tomes. Jane loves history. It's her favorite subject, and she has a brain for remembering dates. If this were any other meet, she'd probably just brush up a bit before bed. But this isn't just another meet. It's Randall High. And she skipped practice. She has to prove herself tomorrow.

Using every ounce of energy left in her body, Jane heaves herself up from her chair and pulls down a book on the Vietnam War. She starts to gather more books, making a fairly sizable pile that seems to make her more and more tired with each addition. Simply brushing up is not an option. This is going to take all night.

• • •

Peas, potatoes, chicken. Peas, potatoes, chicken.

"Meena, would you pass the butter, please?" her mother asks from the end of the table. Without looking up from her full plate, Meena picks up the butter dish and hands it to her mother.

Peas, potatoes, chicken.

She has to concentrate to keep her eyes from wandering. If they do, she knows they'll eventually fall on Steven, who's sitting across from her. And if she looks at him, she'll be sick. She knows he'll have that look on his face. The one that reminds her he knows something about her that no one else does. That they've shared something that no one else can know about.

I'm never doing this again, Meena thinks. *I don't care what Lansky thinks is best for me. I can't sit across the table from Steven and eat. I can't sit here and pretend that nothing has happened.*

All around her are noises of a happy family meal. Her parents chat with Lydia about a big event coming up at the college and Steven chimes in about the role his department will be taking. Trace keeps making mountains out of his potatoes, decorating them with his peas, and calling on the others to look at his work. Utensils clink against china. Lydia laughs her girlish laugh. Platters are passed. Drinks refilled. And every noise, every movement, is like a pinprick against her skin. She feels like she's on display. Like everyone is staring at her—the sullen girl who won't participate. And all she wants to do is get out of here and go up to her room.

"So, Meena . . . how was school today?" her mother asks out of nowhere. The table falls silent. Of course. Someone addressed the freak, and who knows what she'll say?

"Fine," Meena says. *Chicken, peas, potatoes. Chicken,*

peas—

"Please look at me when you're speaking to me," her mother says sternly.

Meena looks left, studiously avoiding any and all eye contact with Steven. "It was fine, Mom," she says flatly.

"Good," her mother answers with a wooden smile nailed to her face.

More silence. Meena looks back down at her plate.

"Well, you're all going to have to count me out for dinner tomorrow night," Meena's father says a bit too brightly. "I have a meeting to attend at school."

"And I'm going to be running a study group," Meena's mother says. "I won't be home till late."

Meena's blood runs cold and she grasps at the thighs of her baggy jeans under the table, pulling the excess material into her sweaty palms. *Both* her parents are going to be out tomorrow night? But that means . . . that means she'll be alone with the Claytons.

I guess I won't be coming home again, she thinks, tears welling up behind her eyes.

"Well! This house is going to be very empty, then!" Lydia says with a laugh. "Steven and I are taking Trace over to the Nicholsons' house. It's their little boy's birthday and we're all getting together."

Suddenly Meena's grip on her jeans disappears. Wait a minute. Does this really mean what she thinks it means?

"Oh," her mother says. "Well, then, Meena . . . I guess

that means you have the house all to yourself."

She sounds skeptical, as if she's unsure whether this is a good idea or not, but Meena doesn't even care. Relief floods her entire body and she actually starts to smile beneath the curtain of her dark hair. All alone in her house! Doing whatever she wants! She can't even remember what it feels like to not have a million eyes on her all at once. To not be judged at every move.

To not be afraid.

"I guess so," Meena says, looking up of her own volition for the first time all night.

"Are you going to be okay?" her mother asks. She rests her elbows on the table and clasps her hands together, looking at Meena like she's a mental patient.

Don't let it bother you, Meena tells herself. *After all, you haven't been acting exactly normal lately.*

"I'll be fine, Mom," she says with a shrug, looking her mother in the eye. "Really. Don't worry about me." Then she takes her first bite of food for good measure just to show her mother how well she's actually doing. She needs this night. She can't let one of them decide to stay home to look after her. Especially not Steven.

"Maybe we should discuss this later," her father says, shooting a meaningful glance at Meena's mom. "The three of us."

"Good idea," her mother says. She smiles reassuringly at Meena. "We'll talk after dinner, okay, Meena?"

Meena bristles, but she forces herself to smile back. She

knows why her parents are concerned. With the fire and the lying and the staying out all night—she knows they think she's lost it.

"Okay," Meena says, taking another bite of her food. She keeps her chin up while studiously avoiding Steven's gaze.

A whole night alone, Meena thinks. All she'll have to do at this little postdinner conversation is convince them she's not going to do anything crazy. And she will convince them. Because she's not going to let Steven take any more of her freedom.

• • •

As Peter waits for Mr. Boyle to return Monday's history exams to the class, he feels an unfamiliar, jittery sensation of anticipation. He can't stop staring at the pile of papers at the edge of Boyle's desk. Boyle reaches toward them, and Peter's heart actually catches. What is wrong with him?

Peter scoffs at himself, shaking his head and looking down at his desk. He's been nervous about getting tests back before, but never like this. This time he's feeling . . . confident. Even psyched.

"Okay, people," Boyle says. He picks up the papers and slaps the pile against his hand. "Time to see how you did."

Peter sits up straight in his chair and tries not to look as freaked as he feels. Mr. Boyle is one of those teachers who always comments as he hands back papers so that everyone in the room is aware of just how sucky your performance was. In the past Peter has gotten such winners as,

"Davis, you never cease to disappoint me," and, "Another dazzling performance!" (Said sarcastically, of course.)

"Mr. Yanofsky!" Boyle announces, pausing next to Matt's desk. "Pitiful!" He slaps the exam down and takes a step.

"Ms. Jolsen!" Tsiliana looks so pale, she could pass out. "Nice work!" Big sigh of relief.

"Mr. Rafferty!" Boyle pauses to shake his head dramatically. "Just . . . see me after class."

Finally, after an agonizingly long time, Boyle makes his way over to Peter's desk. Peter can hear his heart pounding in his ears as he looks up at the paunchy, wrinkly teacher. The man pauses just a tad too long and Peter feels like he's going to drown.

"Mr. Davis," he says, an impressed lilt in his voice. "A vast improvement."

Peter grins as Mr. Boyle places a nearly red-mark–free paper on his desk. There's a tiny B-plus in the corner. Peter just stares at it. A B-plus? In *history?* If he could jump out of his chair and hug the man, he definitely would.

Instead he simply glances over at Danny, who's sitting to his right, lifts the paper, and smiles. Danny smiles right back and gives a little nod.

The bell rings and chairs scrape back as everyone flees. Doug Anderson and Keith Kleiner, however, hover at the front by the blackboard, waiting for Peter to maneuver around the desks.

"What's up?" Peter asks, the B-plus lying in his lap. "Why aren't you guys running for the parking lot?"

"Just wanted to see what you got, Mr. *Vast Improvement*," Doug says, snatching up the paper. He looks at it and laughs. "What's this? The next step in your new stick-up-your-butt deal?"

Peter feels his face heat up and he pushes at his wheels, lurching toward the door. Leave it to his so-called friends to suck any sweetness right out of his moment.

"A B-plus!" Keith exclaims, grabbing the paper. "Dude, you have been hanging out with Jane the Brain way too much."

Doug laughs his slow, deep laugh and slaps hands with Keith as they follow Peter out into the hall. "You're such a loser, Davis," he says. "What's next? Gonna join the glee club?"

"That's it," Peter says under his breath, stopping in the middle of the hallway so that a couple of girls have to dodge their way around him.

"Whadja say . . . *loser?*" Doug teases, still cracking up.

Peter spins his chair around and glares up at them.

"I said, *that's it,*" Peter repeats. "*You guys* are the losers. I mean, why don't you just say what you're really thinking? Ever since my accident you've been acting like total morons around me. So just tell me, okay! Tell me that ever since the accident, I've become totally pointless. It's what you're thinking, isn't it?"

Everyone in the hall falls silent and Doug and Keith look around, knowing that there's not much they can say that won't make them look like bigger creeps than they already do.

"Whatever," Doug says finally, turning and trudging off down the hallway, his massive shoulders hunched.

"Yeah, man, whatever," Keith adds. He tosses Peter's history test back onto his lap. "Call us when you feel like being cool again."

Peter watches Keith take off after Doug and rolls his eyes. Normally he knows he'd feel all tense over having an argument with his friends, but at this moment he actually feels nothing but relief. He's not going to be calling those guys anytime soon.

He glances down at his B-plus and a smile twitches at his lips. He's made a new start. Maybe it's time to make some new friends as well.

● ● ●

Thursday afternoon, Jane walks into the auditorium and heads directly for the stage, where the rest of the school's jazz band is lounging around, eating sandwiches out of brown paper bags. They have a concert coming up and Mr. Vega has called one of his usual emergency lunch rehearsals. Normally she would relish the idea of spending lunch period in the dusky, musty auditorium, hanging with the other band members and playing music. But today is not a normal day. Today is a day following a sleepless night in which her brain had flipped back and forth between history facts and SAT scores all night. It's also a day in which she's totally screwed up a pop quiz and has almost fallen asleep in two classes. She hasn't eaten since yesterday afternoon and she is about ready to collapse.

"Hey," she says to Danny as she hoists herself up onto the stage with a good deal of effort.

"What's up?" Danny says through a mouthful of Twinkie. "You look like death."

"Thanks," Jane says, rolling her eyes as she weakly pulls her lunch out of her backpack. She opens it up, takes one look at the half-mashed tuna sandwich, and puts it aside. She can't even think about eating. Instead she pulls out a bottle of water and sips at it, staring out across the empty seats.

"Something wrong?" Danny asks, pulling his legs up onto the stage and turning to face her. He picks up one of his drumsticks and starts twirling it in his fingers. "Are you still pissed at me?"

Jane scoffs. She hasn't thought about the tape since the moment it left her hands. There have been too many other things cramming her mind, jockeying for her attention.

"I just came from a quiz in French and I was so tired, I kept answering all the questions in Spanish," she tells him.

Danny laughs and Jane shoots him a withering glare. Danny's mouth snaps shut. "Sorry," he says. "But come on, you're Jane Scott. I bet you can afford to biff one quiz. They'll probably give you an A out of habit."

Jane feels a sudden, inexplicable desire to strangle Danny Chaiken. He doesn't get it. No one gets it. It's not just one quiz. It's just another in a long line of failures. Jane is just barely holding it together. And all the while the SAT scores are there. Looming. Mocking her from under her mattress. Sooner or later they're going to have to come out. And what is she going to do then? What will Danny and all the other people who think of her as Miss Perfect say then?

Just tell them. Tell somebody. Get it out there. Then they'll stop. Stop pestering you. Stop expecting things of you.

Part of her feels that it would be a relief. A huge relief if everyone stopped expecting her to be perfect. But another part of her—a bigger part—doesn't know what would be left. Who would she be if she wasn't an overachiever?

But you're not *an overachiever. Not anymore.*

"Let's get started, people!" Mr. Vega calls out, all business, snapping Jane out of her morose thoughts. He taps his conductor's baton on his music stand and everyone scrambles to their feet, tossing garbage in the cans at the sides of the stage. Jane launches her brown bag into one of them, grabs her sax case, and heads for her chair.

When she sits down, she realizes she's the only one who hasn't put together her instrument yet. Her heart fluttering with nervousness, Jane pulls out her sax and rushes to attach the reed and mouthpiece. In the process her case clatters to the floor, taking her music stand over with it. Jane turns nine shades of red as the rest of the jazz band applauds her dexterity.

"Can we begin, Ms. Scott?" Mr. Vega says, arching one eyebrow.

Jane mutters an apology, glancing fretfully at the director. Normally he's a perfectly nice, genial guy, but the second he gets up there to conduct, he becomes a heartless slave driver. It's a classic Dr. Jekyll and Mr. Hyde scenario.

"We'll be starting today with 'All That Jazz,'" Mr. Vega announces, causing a huge ruffling of papers.

Jane isn't listening, however. She's too busy trying to organize everything and quell her embarrassment. She finally gets her instrument together and rights her music stand. By the time Mr. Vega lifts his arms to begin, she's ready.

She takes a deep breath just before he gives the cue and begins to play. Just a few notes in, Jane realizes something is horribly wrong. Her notes are dissonant and she's totally off tempo. Everyone stops playing gradually and looks at her. By this point Jane is frozen in her chair, realizing she's been playing the wrong piece.

Her empty stomach ties into knots as Mr. Vega glares down at her. "What piece did I request, Ms. Scott?" he asks.

Jane glances at her music stand, reads the title of the song she'd been playing—the song they've been starting their rehearsals with for the last month. Of course, he had to choose today to change it. And she had to be flustered enough to miss it.

"I'm guessing it wasn't 'Dream a Little Dream,'" she says, hoping for a mood-breaking laugh. She gets it, but only from a few students.

"Not even close," he says humorlessly. "Let's see if you can get it right this time."

Embarrassed beyond belief, Jane rifles through her music,

looking for "All That Jazz"—the piece she recognized the rest of the band playing. Mr. Vega has never yelled at her before, though, and it has her totally thrown. She can barely grasp the pages, her fingers are shaking so badly. She manages to go through her pile twice to no avail. *Where is it?* she wails silently, aware that all eyes are on her. *Come on. Come on.*

"Here," Missy Zambias whispers from the next chair, handing over the music. "I have an extra."

"Well, then, now that we've wasted five minutes of everyone's lunch period . . . shall we?" Mr. Vega raises his arms again and begins to conduct.

Jane can barely play, but she does the best she can to avoid having Mr. Vega come down on her again. Tears threaten to overflow, but she won't let them. All she wants to do is get out of here, but even when she imagines herself running through the auditorium doors, she can't imagine where she would go. Every single place would offer just as much stress as where she is right now. And so she just plays through her tears.

Plays and prays she won't mess up.

CHAPTER NiNE

Don't let it *be a history question. Anything but history . . . please!*

Jane sits in her chair in Ms. Motti's room for the Academic Decathlon meet on Thursday afternoon, clenching and unclenching her hands in her lap. Her brain keeps repeating all the questions she's missed this afternoon, and there have been quite a few. With each missed answer the classroom has seemed to get smaller and smaller, the air warmer and warmer. By the time the final round begins, Jane is drenched with sweat and holding her breath.

I just want to get out of here. I just need to—

"Falls High, your last question is in . . . history," the proctor says in her pinched voice. Jane feels her teammates tense up around her and realizes that they don't trust her.

And why would they? Jane thinks as she rises out of her chair, pulling down on the hem of her gray sweatshirt. *You've missed questions a sixth grader could have answered.*

"Okay, Miss Scott. If you answer this correctly, your

team wins. If not, the meet goes to Randall High." The woman's curly black hair trembles when she speaks, like something alive. Jane can't help thinking she'd make a good evil, mythical creature. "Your question, Miss Scott: In what year was the tomb of King Tutankhamen discovered?"

Huh? Is she kidding? Jane wonders, panic seizing her heart.

"You have thirty seconds," the proctor says. The big digital clock on the teacher's desk starts to count down.

I don't need thirty seconds! Jane wants to scream, wringing her hands into her sweatshirt. *I have no idea and in thirty seconds I'm still going to have no idea.*

Her teammates start to squirm and none of them will look at her. She knows that they know they're all doomed. How could they have asked her such an obscure question?

Okay, just think. You know it was in the twentieth century and it wasn't in your lifetime. A bead of sweat runs along her temple to her ear. *It was probably before World War II since that's when all the major digs went on in Egypt.*

She glances at the clock. There are six seconds left. She sucks in a sharp breath, glances at the smirking faces of the Randall High team, and takes a stab in the dark.

"1924?"

There's an audible groan from behind her. Ms. Motti's groan.

"I'm sorry," the proctor says, sounding anything but. "It was 1922. The meet goes to Randall High!"

Suddenly the room is filled with a cacophony of shouts, applause, moving chairs, and laughter. Jane just stands there as the Randall High team celebrates and most of her teammates rush quickly out of the room, exasperated and disappointed. Jane catches plenty of withering looks. She feels as though her knees are going to give out at any second.

Taking one step back, Jane falls into her chair and tries not to burst into tears as she packs up her stuff. She can't believe this is happening. She can't believe it's her fault they lost the meet. Jane has never missed so many questions in her life.

I'm a failure. I'm a failure. She imagines the inevitable phone call from her father tonight. Hears herself lying. She'll tell him they lost, but she won't tell him why.

"You okay?" Regina Thurber asks, pausing in front of Jane's chair.

Jane just shrugs. She can't trust herself to talk without sobbing.

"Hey, don't worry about it," Regina says. "No one knew the answer to that one."

Yeah, but I bet everyone knew the answers to all the other stupid questions I missed.

"Thanks," Jane says, mentally willing her to walk away like everyone else has.

Regina glances past Jane's shoulder and blinks as if she sees someone coming. Someone she doesn't want to talk to. "So, I'll see you later," she says, then quickly makes her escape.

The chair next to Jane's moves and squeals and Jane recognizes the tangy scent of Ms. Motti's perfume.

"I've never seen such a sorry performance out of you, Jane," she snaps.

"I'm sorry. I just had an off day," Jane says, keeping her back to the teacher as she zips up her backpack.

Just go away! she thinks. *Go away and leave me alone with my total failure!*

"Well, you'd better get your act together before the championship match," Ms. Motti continues. "We haven't lost the championships since before Quinn Saunders was captain and I'm not about to start now."

Quinn Saunders. Jane feels the name all over her body. It makes her skin tingle and, at the same time, infuses every pore with an overwhelming sense of guilt and disappointment. Quinn had been a senior when Jane was a freshman and she'd idolized him. Loved him. Followed him around in sheer pathetic worship. And still, he'd always been nice to her. Always treated her like an equal instead of one of his many annoying admirers.

Jane had wanted to be just like him—almost as much as she'd wanted to kiss him. Quinn had been in practically every club, played on the lacrosse team, worked at his father's hardware store, and had always seemed perfectly together. He'd been able to juggle more activities and commitments than anyone Jane had ever known, and he'd done it like it was no big deal. Like it was just life and he loved it.

I wish I could be like that, Jane thinks as Ms. Motti pushes herself out of her chair. *I would give anything just to feel calm for five seconds.*

She knows Quinn didn't have a panic attack at his SATs. He had, in fact, gotten a perfect score. Quinn had never failed at one thing in his entire life.

She rises, hoisting her ever-heavy backpack onto her back, and doesn't notice that Sumit is waiting for her by the door until she's almost past him.

"Hey, you all right?" he asks.

"I'm fine," Jane says, even though her body feels exhausted and her mind keeps repeating the name King Tutankhamen over and over again. "You want to lecture me, too?"

"No," Sumit says. "I just . . . I think you should get some rest. You look really tired."

Hearing someone else say it makes her want to collapse right there. She has a momentary vision of falling into Sumit's arms and snoring against his sweater vest.

"Thanks," she says, moving away from him. "But I took Reed's shift today, so I have to get to work."

"Well, don't fall asleep in the yogurt machine!" Sumit calls after her good-naturedly.

I won't, Jane thinks. *I'll be too busy studying.*

• • •

Reed stands at the end of the kitchen table and stares down at the rows of certificates he's laid out there. They're all very similar—white parchment paper with colored borders

146

and his name written in calligraphy across a line in the center. They proclaim Reed to be a National Merit Scholar, Student of the Year, National Honor Society Member, Science Student of the Year, and on and on.

He hasn't seen any of these certificates since the awards ceremonies at which he received them.

As soon as Reed had arrived home after practice today, he'd ransacked the house, looking for the awards—trying to figure out where his mother had stashed them. Ironically, they'd been stored in the drawers underneath the cabinet where all T. J.'s trophies are proudly displayed, dusted and buffed on a weekly basis by the cleaning woman who visits the house.

The front door closes and Reed tenses up, all the blood in his body rushing to his face. He hears the click of his mother's heels against the tiles in the foyer and prepares himself. She'll either go up to her room or come to the kitchen for a glass of water. He has to know what he's going to say if she chooses the latter.

The clicks get closer and closer and then his mother pushes through the swinging door into the kitchen, a whirl of silk and heavy perfume.

"Reed!" she blurts out. "What are you doing?"

"Are you proud of me, Mom?" Reed asks, his pulse pounding.

"What?" Her smile falters as her eyes travel down to the table. "What's this about?" she asks uncertainly, taking a step closer and picking up one of the awards. She glances over it and then replaces it, barely seeming to register what she's seen.

Reed doesn't move a muscle. Doesn't even blink. "Are you proud of me?"

"Well, yes. Of course," she says, her complexion growing pink. "You know I am."

"Then why are all my awards stashed in a drawer?" Reed asks, clutching the back of the chair in front of him. "T. J.'s are all in the display case. Why are mine hidden?"

"Reed . . . honey . . . there's just no room—"

"Are you kidding me?" Reed scoffs. "Why don't you *make* room? Put away T. J.'s peewee football trophies so that you can put this out?" He holds up the National Merit Scholarship certificate. "This is actually significant, you know? I'd think it could take the place of some yards-earned trophy T. J. won when he was nine."

"There's no need to get sarcastic, Reed," his mother says, lifting her chin slightly.

"I'm sorry, Mom, but do you have any idea how it makes me feel to find these things stuffed in a drawer?" Reed says, gathering the papers up in a pile.

His mother takes a deep breath and lowers herself into a chair. She glances up at Reed, her expression calming, but it has no effect on him. He knows what's coming and it just winds him up more tightly.

"Reed, you know that T. J. needs affirmation more than you do," she says evenly. "Everything has always come so easily for you, and it's a blessing. But T. J. has to work so hard just to get through things that are nothing for you."

As if I haven't worked for the awards I've won, Reed thinks. He opens his mouth to say just that, but his mother cuts him off.

"You know, I've always admired you for being so understanding of your big brother," she says with a small smile. "A lot of children would have lashed out or put him down, but you were never like that, Reed. You've never flaunted your talents in front of T. J. Never made him feel less than you are. Do you know how admirable that is?"

Reed's jaw clenches. He knows what she's trying to do. She's trying to tell him to just let it go. Let things continue the way they always have been. And as ridiculous as it is, he knows T. J. would be hurt if he came home to find the trophy case rearranged. It's his pride and joy.

Reed's heart pangs with guilt and he looks down at the pile of certificates. He wants to tell his mother that the trophy case doesn't matter. He just wants her to recognize what he's achieved. But he can't. It sounds too whiny in his head. So instead, he just picks up the papers and walks out of the room.

• • •

Peter looks up from his physics book for the first time in over an hour and is surprised to see that his room is filled with shadows. His desk lamp is shining down on the glossy pages and he doesn't even remember turning it on. He rubs at his eyes, making everything blurry, and pushes himself back from the desk. His brain feels like mush.

149

"So this is what studying feels like," he says aloud with a chuckle. "Weird."

He glances out the window and notices that the fading sun is putting on a fairly impressive light show, so he turns his chair and wheels himself over for a better view. But the closer he gets to the window, the more he can see of the blackened remains of the Claytons' house. It's a stark contrast, the charred slabs of wood jutting in all directions against the pink-and-gold sky.

I can't believe Meena was actually in there when that happened, Peter thinks, a shudder going through him. He wonders how someone can live through that and not have nightmares for the rest of their life.

Maybe they can't, he realizes. *I'm still having nightmares about . . .*

He shakes his head. He doesn't want to go there. Not now. He turns his thoughts back to Meena and wonders how she's doing—where she is at that very moment. His mind conjures a picture of Meena sitting on a window seat in her room, reading a book. He has no idea what her bedroom looks like, but in his mind's eye it's basic and nongirly. She's totally engrossed in what she's reading, but the moment Peter walks in, she looks up and smiles a familiar smile.

Peter glances down at his legs. Maybe he should imagine himself rolling in. Be realistic. But then, it's *his* daydream. He can fly in if he wants to.

He leans back in his chair and takes it a step further. He

and Meena walk together, hand in hand, through the halls at school. All Peter's former friends gape at him as she laughs and leans her head on his shoulder. They study in the library together, run to her car to head out for lunch, cuddle on the school steps before school.

Then, unbidden, he sees himself waiting at the bottom of the staircase at Meena's house in a black tuxedo. His heart catches in his chest when she appears at the top of the stairs in a long, light blue gown. She walks down the stairs slowly, looking at him like he's the only guy in the world. And just as the imaginary Meena leans in to kiss him, Peter feels a familiar warmth overcome his body. It starts in his scalp and then tingles its way down his neck, over his shoulders, and down his arms.

This time, instead of wondering what it is—where it's coming from—Peter just lets himself drift through the warmth, overcome by the soothing sensation and the imagined touch of Meena's lips. Before he knows it, he's smiling as he starts to doze off, floating off in a haze.

And just before he falls asleep, he feels it. He knows he does. There's a tingling in his legs.

• • •

"What *is* this?" the foul-faced man in the too-tight denim jacket shouts at Jane. He holds out his overflowing cup of sprinkle-covered yogurt and scowls, but Jane can't even seem to get her vision to focus. "Were you even listening when we ordered? I said vanilla, not *coconut*."

Jane feels an intense hatred for this person bubble up inside her chest and wonders, vaguely, how her spent body can handle such a fierce emotion.

"I'll fix it," she says, wiping her arm across her forehead. She snatches the cup away from the man and he starts to bitch to his girlfriend as she chucks it toward the garbage can. She's too tired to make it, though, and the whole thing hits the floor, splattering yogurt in all directions.

"Jane! What are you doing?" her manager, Peggy, shrieks, emerging from the back office. She glances at the enraged customers, then at the mess and then at Jane. "Clean that up. I'll take care of the customers."

"Fine," Jane says through her teeth. She heads into the back room for the mop and notices that her hands are shaking uncontrollably as she opens the closet. She swallows hard, pulls out the mop, and takes a deep breath, trying to calm her nerves.

Only a couple more hours, she tells herself. She doesn't even let herself think of all the things she has to do when she gets home.

But why? her mind asks, the little voice in her head sounding oddly far away. *Why are you going to bother doing all those things? Why, why, why, why, why . . . ?*

When she pushes her way back into the restaurant, the scary toad man and his girlfriend are gone and Reed is walking through the front door. Jane doesn't even say hello. It feels like it will take up too much energy. She crouches behind the counter, holding the splintery mop handle with one hand while she picks up the fallen styrofoam cup with the other. Reed comes around the counter just as she starts to stand, giving herself a massive head rush. Everything goes fuzzily gray and Jane glances at Reed, waiting for it to clear.

But it doesn't. *This is not good,* Jane thinks absently. She blinks once, her stomach heaves, Reed's face goes pale, and then everything is black.

" . . . an ambulance or her parents . . . ? I have her number right here if we . . . Oh man, she just went down like a sack of potatoes. . . . Thank God you were here."

Jane's head is lying on something soft, but the rest of her body hurts like crazy. She feels a hand on her forehead. Thinks of her father. Then tunes in to the voices.

"Peggy, I think she needs air," one voice says calmly. "Maybe you should just take a step back."

"Okay, I'll call her parents."

"No!" Jane shouts. A stabbing pain pierces her temple and she gasps for air. It takes all the effort in the world, but she manages to open her eyes. Somehow that brings the three identical faces she sees before her together into one. "Don't call my parents, please," she croaks, her throat completely dry.

"Jane? Are you okay?" The voice belongs to Reed, whose lap her head is apparently resting in. "Do you want some water?"

She nods just the slightest bit. Hears the faucet bang on. The shoosh of the water. Then Peggy hands the little plastic cup to Reed and he holds it in front of her. She lifts her head up carefully. The pain happens again, but it's less. The water feels like heaven going down.

"What happened?" she asks, closing her eyes against the harsh fluorescent light.

"I think you fainted," Reed says. "You just went down."

"Oh . . . that's weird," Jane says, because she feels like she should say something. She looks up at Peggy, who's standing there with a look of sheer uncertainty and fear on her face. "Don't call my parents," Jane says. "They have enough to deal with right now."

"Well, you should go home," Peggy says. "You can't work in this condition."

"No. It's okay," Jane says, bracing her arms on the floor. Reed's hands instantly support her back. "I can get up—"

Reed gets to his feet and helps her stand, lifting her almost the whole way. But the moment she's up again, her head swims, and she has to lean into his side for support. She glances up at his profile, feeling like a complete loser. What kind of person can't even make it through a shift without fainting?

"Why don't I take you home?" Reed suggests, his arm around her shoulders. Even if she's embarrassed, it's oddly comforting, being taken care of.

"Okay," Jane says, realizing she's not going to be much good in her groggy, shaky state. "Thanks, Reed." She glances at Peggy weakly. "Are you going to be okay here by yourself?"

"Don't worry about it," she says. "It's slow tonight anyway."

As Reed helps Jane out of the store, Peggy calls after her that she hopes she'll feel better, but Jane doesn't answer. All she can think about is how she's going to explain her early arrival—sans car—to her mother. And how she's going to get all her work done when she's exhausted enough to faint. And how she's going to practice her sax when she feels like her skull is going to crack open.

Why am I doing this? her groggy brain asks again. *Why, why, why, why, why . . . ?*

CHAPTER TEN

"So . . . I guess I should thank you for . . . catching me," Jane says as she climbs into the passenger seat of Reed's car. Her whole body relaxes as she settles into the well-worn cushions. "What were you doing there, anyway?"

"I came to get my paycheck," Reed says. "I'm just glad I got behind the counter in time," he adds. "I don't think Peggy's reflexes would've kicked in as fast."

Jane blows out a weak laugh through her nose and turns her head to stare through the window. She barely has the energy to keep her eyes open, but she refuses to fall asleep on Reed.

"Jane, do you mind me asking . . . is everything okay?" Reed asks as he pulls the car out into traffic. "You don't look so good."

"Well, I did just faint," Jane says, keeping her eyes trained on the passing scenery. Her mind is still asking the question over and over again. It's getting louder. *Why, why, why . . . ?*

"Yeah, well, that's what I mean," Reed says. "Are you sick or something?"

Jane squeezes her eyes closed and sighs. She knows that Reed means well, but there's no way he could possibly understand what's going on in her life. There's no way he could comprehend the stress, the heavy guilt she constantly has weighing down on her chest. Reed has the perfect life. He's wealthy, popular, athletic, and he has a perfect mom and an even more perfect brother. She's sure he's never sweated a day in his life.

Kind of like Quinn, Jane thinks, then immediately wants to shake her head at herself. Ever since Ms. Motti mentioned Quinn this afternoon, he's been popping up in her thoughts.

"I don't really want to talk about it," Jane says. She leans back in her seat and glances at him out of the corner of her eye. "No offense. I'm just kind of tired."

"That's all right," Reed says, watching the road. "But if you ever want to—"

"Do you have any idea how Quinn Saunders is doing?" Jane asks, more than ready to change the subject. Reed always seems to know what everyone is doing with their lives, probably because either he or someone in his family is friends with practically everyone in town.

"Quinn?" Reed's brow furrows as he comes to a stop at a red light. "I think I heard he transferred out of Stanford after his freshman year, but I don't know where he ended up. Why?"

Jane blinks, confused. Quinn and Stanford are practically

synonymous in her mind. The guy never talked about going anywhere else. Why would he transfer out of his dream school after only one year?

Why, why, why, why, why . . . ?

"Jane?" Reed prompts.

She blushes a deep crimson and looks down at her lap. "Oh, it's just Motti mentioned him today and I hadn't thought about him in a while, so . . ."

Lie. She thinks about Quinn all the time, when she's not thinking about all of the work she has to do. He must have transferred to someplace like Harvard or Oxford. Probably didn't feel challenged enough at a plain old *impossibly hard* school like Stanford.

"You know, Quinn's little sister, Faith, is having a party next weekend," Reed says as the light turns green. "You should come and ask Faith what the deal is. I mean . . . if you're really curious."

A burst of laughter escapes Jane's lips and hangs in the air, surprising them both. Jane hadn't thought her catatonic body was capable of making such a sound.

"What's so funny?" Reed asks.

"Me. At Faith Saunders's party." She looks at him, incredulous, and he responds with a blank glance. "Don't you have to fulfill some popularity quotient to get into those things?" she says sarcastically.

Now it's Reed's turn to laugh. "Whatever," he says. "Jane, you're not unpopular."

Jane's pretty sure it's the greatest compliment she's ever received. Reed Frasier, arguably the king of the school, doesn't see her as unpopular. Weird.

"Yeah, but I'm not *popular*," Jane says.

Reed pulls into her driveway and puts the car in park, then turns to look her squarely in the eye. "I'll bet you money that if you show up at that party, people will be happy to see you. Surprised, but happy."

Jane forces a smile, but her thoughts are no longer on Quinn and Faith and her own popularity. She's home. Early. With no car. And no SAT scores.

"Thanks for the ride," she says, getting out with her many bags.

As Reed backs out of the driveway, Jane watches his car, trying to figure out what to say to her mom.

Maybe my car broke down, she thinks as she trudges her exhausted self up to the door. *I can tell her it wouldn't start and then tomorrow when we go to get it, it'll be like a miracle. Oh my gosh! I can't believe it started!*

She opens the front door ever so quietly. Closes it with the slightest click. Then, holding her breath, she tiptoes double time up to her room and slips inside. Her bed is the loveliest thing she's ever seen.

Dropping her bags on the floor, Jane waits for a moment and listens. She doesn't hear her mother stirring. Unreal. She's done it. She's actually snuck in undetected. With a sigh of relief, Jane kicks off her shoes, lies down on top of her bed, pulls the covers over her body, and waits for sleep.

But the moment she closes her eyes, she sees Ms. Motti's harsh face, hears Mr. Vega's angry voice, sees all the cross-outs on her French test, pictures her SAT scores under her mattress, her parents' imminent disappointment.

The voice in her mind is louder than ever. *Why are you doing this? Why do you keep pretending when it's all going to come out eventually? Why, why, why . . . ?*

• • •

"I am the master!" Danny calls out in the middle of the crowded arcade, throwing his hands into the air. He's just beaten Cori in the NASCAR simulator for the second time. He'd won the first race and she'd won the second, but he dusted her by a mile in the third. Which means he's won their bet—best two out of three. Which also means he is not going to have to brave The Electrifier.

"I won!" Danny gloats, grinning at Cori.

"Yes. I know you won," Cori returns, rolling her eyes but smiling.

Danny lets out a little "whoop!" There's not much he likes more than winning.

"Just say it," Danny tells Cori, clapping. "Just say, 'Danny is the master.'"

Cori rolls her eyes again but grins. "Not in this lifetime, Chaiken."

"Hey, don't be a sore loser," Danny tells her, shoving his

hands in the pocket on the front of his sweatshirt. "The bet was your idea."

"I know, I know," Cori says. She sidesteps a couple of kids who are tearing through the arcade toward the skeeball games and pauses in front of The Electrifier. "Whoever came up with this thing is sick," she says, eyeing the chair warily. It's not even a game. It's just a chair that gives a person increasingly intense electric shocks until they can't take it anymore, then awards tickets based on how long the person endures the torture.

"Again, your idea," Danny says with a shrug as he bounces up and down on the balls of his feet. "But hey, if you want to back out . . ."

"There's one thing you should know about me," Cori says, slipping out of her leather jacket and handing it to Danny. "Once I say I'm going to do something, I never back out."

She looks him deep in the eyes as she says it and Danny feels his already frayed nerves sizzle even more.

What is up with my medication? he wonders, gripping the jacket in his sweaty fist. Night before last, when the fog had returned, Danny had thought that was it. That it was going to be all foggy all the time. And he'd tried to mentally prepare himself for it. So why was today so up and down? Why had he been fine in school and why is he losing it now?

I gotta talk to Lansky about this, he thinks. *Maybe it's kicking in gradually . . . ?*

Danny shakes his head when he realizes he's actually wishing for the numbness the fog brings. In this particular situation, feeling nothing would be better than this ready-to-burst thing.

The last thing he wants is to do something stupid in front of Cori . . . *again*. Especially after having to practically offer up his firstborn to get permission to come tonight. But he'd managed to convince his parents that dealing with being back on the meds would be easier if he wasn't just sitting in his room obsessing. And once he'd shown them proof that all his homework was done, they'd caved—*with* a strict early curfew, of course.

He takes a deep breath as Cori slides her prepaid game card through The Electrifier and sits down. The thing kicks into gear, making a buzzing noise that sounds not unlike a chain saw. The longer she sits, the more little lights above her head blink on. Suddenly Danny notices she's holding her breath.

"You okay?" he asks, a bit of irrational fear gripping his heart. They wouldn't put a machine that was actually dangerous in here, would they?

"Fine," Cori responds, her voice slightly strained. Her hair starts to stick up and it's all Danny can do to keep from pulling her out of there.

She's fine, he tells himself. *Just chill.*

Finally, when almost all the lights are shining, Cori stands up. "Ugh! Never again!" she says, shaking out her arms. A ton of little yellow tickets comes spewing out of the machine.

"I'm impressed," Danny says, his heart pounding as he hands her jacket back. There are little beads of sweat forming along his hairline, so he wipes them away with his sleeve. "What are you gonna get with those?"

Cori leans down to grab her tickets and Danny pulls his sweatshirt off, exposing the white T-shirt underneath. The sudden blast of cold air that hits his arms serves to calm him just a bit.

"Maybe I can get a whole eraser!" Cori says with fake giddiness. She starts for the prize counter.

"This sucks," Danny says, looking through the glass counter at mugs worth four hundred tickets. "You'd probably have to spend fifty bucks on games just to get a mug." He feels his fists balling up and tries to ignore it.

"Oh, look! I can get a spider ring!" Cori says with a grin. She slaps her tickets down on the counter and thrusts out her hand. The incredibly bored-looking kid hands her a plastic spider ring and Cori holds it up between her thumb and forefinger, gazing at it like it's a rare diamond.

Danny laughs and leans on the counter, going for casual. "So? Put it on," he says.

"You do it," Cori says, holding the ring out to him. "I've always wondered what it would be like to have a guy slip a ring on my finger," she adds jokingly.

Danny's heart skips a few beats. Is she flirting with him?

He stands up straight as she holds out her hand. He's

163

shaking as he slips the little plastic band over her finger, but he manages to look her right in the eye the whole time. And she's smiling. Smiling flirtatiously.

"So?" he says once the ring is in place. "How did it feel?"

Oh God! Did I really just say that? I'm such a moron! I'm so stupid. She's going to laugh her ass off. She's going to—

"Kinda nice, actually," she says, holding her hand up to inspect the ring. Then she grabs his arm and nearly pulls him off his feet. "Let's eat!"

A little while later he's sitting across from her in a hard plastic booth, eating onion rings and trying to stop his legs from bouncing up and down beneath the table. He keeps finding himself looking around the room—at the game area, the snack bar, the dirty rug—everywhere but at Cori.

It's getting worse. He needs to figure out some way to calm down. He grabs a napkin out of the metal dispenser on the table and starts to shred it into tiny bits. When he glances up, Cori is watching him closely and Danny starts to sweat again. She knows he's freaking.

But how can she? She doesn't even know I'm bipolar. She thinks I'm just a normal guy.

"Are you all right?" she asks, putting her burger down.

"I'm fine!" Danny blurts out. Then he clears his throat, thinking about the night before last. Thinking about how, before he'd screwed everything up, he'd been so content. He'd been listening to her voice, calm and happy. Foggy, but calm and happy.

She knows . . . she knows, she knows, she knows. He clasps and unclasps his hands, trying to keep himself from rocking forward and back like his body seems to want to do.

"So . . . uh . . . what did that chair thing feel like, anyway?" he asks, hoping that if he can get her talking, she won't notice that he's sweating and freaking.

She eyes him and for a moment he's sure she's going to ask him something else, but then she seems to think better of it and just starts to talk. "Well, it was fine when it started. It just felt like a little tingle. But then . . ."

Danny tries to focus, but he can't. All he can think about is the overwhelming guilt that's settling in on his shoulders. Guilt over lying to Cori about who he really is. Guilt over blaming his sisters for the accident. Guilt over stopping his medication, because if he hadn't, he wouldn't be feeling like this right now and he wouldn't be on the verge of ruining a perfectly fun night.

"I need to go," Danny says, pulling his sweatshirt off the bench next to him and yanking it on over his head.

"What? Why?" Cori asks. She has a french fry halfway to her mouth as she looks at him, clearly disappointed and concerned.

"I can't . . . I can't. . . ." He squeezes his eyes shut, realizing he sounds psychotic.

"Danny—"

"I have to get out of here!" he shouts. Then, feeling his stomach lurch, Danny turns and bolts through the arcade.

• • •

"This is the life," Meena says to her empty house on Thursday evening. She almost laughs at herself. She can't remember the last time she felt remotely comfortable, let alone content.

Just go with it, she tells herself. *Enjoy it while it lasts . . . because it won't last long.*

She sits down on the couch in the living room and looks around, wondering when it was that she'd last sat here. She's been spending so much time hiding out in her room or roaming the streets, she's not sure if she's hung out in her living room at all in the last few weeks. It doesn't look different, but it *feels* different.

But then, it's Meena who has changed.

A little pang stops Meena's heart. It's almost nostalgic. Like she's remembering a friend she's lost. But she manages to swipe away the feeling. She's not going to have any sad thoughts tonight. She's just going to sit here and watch TV like she's a normal person.

Meena clicks on the television set, lifts up her ponytail so that it falls behind the back of the couch, and pulls her cozy blue sweatshirt closer to her body as she snuggles back into the cushions. She's just starting to let out a comfortable sigh when a car pulls into the driveway.

Meena bolts up, clutching the remote. She manages to lift a shaky hand and hit the mute button. Yep. It's in her driveway. The engine sounds like it's in her own head.

Maybe it's just Mom or Dad, she thinks, running to the window. But it's Steven's car. And he's alone.

Meena runs to the kitchen and grabs the phone, her heart slamming against her rib cage. *Why is he here? Why is he here? Why is he here?* her mind repeats over and over. Steven is supposed to be out with his family. And her parents won't be home for hours.

This can't be happening. Meena looks down at the little numbers on the telephone as the dial tone assaults her ears. Who does she think she's going to call, 911? They'd think she was insane. There's no emergency here. At least not to the outside world.

His footsteps crunch along the front path and Meena's eyes dart around. They finally fall on her backpack. Clutching the phone in one hand, she grabs her bag and runs to the stairs, taking them two at a time. Once inside her room, she locks the door and rips open her bag, searching for a little scrap of paper.

The front door closes just as she finds it. She dials the number and holds the phone to her ear, shaking.

"Meena?" Steven calls from downstairs.

Meena squeezes her eyes shut.

The phone clicks. "Hello?"

"Peter?" she whispers. "It's Meena. Can you come over here?"

There's a pause that seems to last a lifetime. "What's wrong?"

"I can't explain," she says desperately, glancing at her bedroom door. "I just need you to come. Please. Please just come over."

The doorknob turns and clicks. A sob escapes her throat and she hits the off button on the phone, dropping it on the bed.

"Meena? I know you're in there," Steven says.

The door rattles and Meena backs away toward the corner of her room, lowers herself onto the floor.

"Meena, sweetie, you can't keep me locked out forever," he says. "I know you've been avoiding me, and you don't know how that hurts. You made me believe we had something."

Meena curls up into a ball and sobs silently, clutching her hands around her legs.

"Fine," he says. "I'm not giving up, Meena. We're all alone here, and that lock won't keep me out forever."

Meena pulls herself in closer as Steven walks back downstairs. What does he mean? Is he going to break into her room? Why won't he just leave her alone?

Please, Peter, get here, she begs silently. *Get here.*

• • •

As Peter's mother pulls her car to a stop in front of Meena's house, all Peter wants to do is run to the front door and break it down. But he can't, of course. He can't even get out of his seat until his mother unpacks his wheelchair and helps him out.

"Dammit," he says under his breath as his mom gets out

of the car. He stares at the silent front of the house, willing it to tell him what's going on inside. He searches the windows and sees nothing. He remembers the sound Meena made just before she hung up. The strangled, scared sob. Panicked, Peter leans over the driver's seat and honks the car horn to let her know, at least, that he's there. It's really, *really* loud.

"Peter!" his mother says as she opens his door. "What do you think you're doing?"

"I'm sorry! I just wanted to let her know I'm here," Peter says through his teeth. He lifts his legs out one at a time and then clutches his mother's arms as she pulls him out of the car.

"First you make me bring you over here without an explanation," she mutters as he plops into the wheelchair. "And now you're disturbing the whole neighborhood—"

"I'm *sorry*, Mom," Peter says, grabbing the wheels on his chair.

Without a backward glance, he swings the chair around and whips himself up Meena's front walk faster than he's ever moved in his chair before. Just as he's about to reach for the doorbell, the door swings open and Meena's standing there. Her eyes are swollen and wet and her face is all red and blotchy. She wears a huge smile that looks morbidly comical against the rest of her features.

"Peter!" she says loudly, clutching the doorknob with both hands. "Thank you *so* much for bringing over my Spanish notes!"

"What the hell is going on?" Peter whispers, glancing

behind her to see if he can figure out who she's putting on an act for.

She looks at him, her eyes pleading, and Peter realizes he has a role to play.

"Oh! No problem!" he says, hopefully sounding natural. "Since I'm here, we might as well . . . study . . . together?" he asks.

Meena's whole frame seems to sag with relief. "Come on in," she tells him.

Peter looks back at his mother, who's standing next to the idling car, hugging herself against the cold. "Thanks, Mom!" he calls out. "Meena will drive me home later."

"Okay, sweetie," his mother says. She's back in the car instantly. Peter says a silent thank-you. For once in his life he's glad his mother is not taking an interest.

The instant Peter is through the door, he sees Steven Clayton standing at the other end of the foyer and he grips his armrests, startled. Peter looks at Meena, noting the panic in her eyes. Is Mr. Clayton somehow the reason she was freaking out earlier? The reason she's now stiff as a board and staring at the floor as she clutches her arms around herself?

"If you'll excuse me," Mr. Clayton says out of nowhere. Then he brushes by Peter and walks through the front door, slamming it behind him. Moments later a car starts up and then peels out, leaving Peter and Meena in total silence. The air is charged with emotion.

Peter has a sickening feeling deep in the pit of his stomach.

He looks up at Meena and a single tear spills down her cheek. It's clear that she's afraid of Steven Clayton. Deathly afraid. And Peter doesn't even want to let himself imagine why.

"Meena," he says hoarsely. "What's going on?"

She shakes her head. More tears. She pulls her hand inside the sleeve of her sweatshirt and holds it to her nose.

The sickening feeling intensifies. It's all Peter can feel. Every other part of him is numb with dread. "Did that guy . . . ? Did he . . . *do* something to you?"

Suddenly Meena bursts into uncontrollable, racking sobs. Her tiny little body seems to convulse as she gasps for air. Peter clenches his fists as the horrifying possibilities crowd his mind, each more sickening than the next. Whatever Steven Clayton has done to Meena, it's clearly ripping her apart, which makes Peter want to rip *him* apart. How could anyone hurt her?

Peter would give anything to be able to stand up and hug Meena. To tell her that everything is going to be all right. But he can't. And from her tight, scared body language, he's not sure she'd want to be touched. All he can do is sit there and listen to her cry. And wish he had the power to hunt down Steven Clayton and kick his ass.

CHAPTER ELEVEN

Jane can barely keep her head up as she trudges her way to the guidance office Friday morning. She hadn't had the energy to actually dress that morning, so comfort clothing in the form of sweats had seemed like a good idea. Big mistake. All day she's felt like she's in her pajamas, which doesn't help with the whole staying-awake-in-class problem.

Jane looks down at the little piece of paper Mrs. Carruthers sent to her English class, requesting her presence. She knows why her guidance counselor wants to see her—she's supposed to have at least three college applications done. But she doesn't. She hasn't filled out a single one.

Why should I? Jane wonders. *Why, when they're all going to see my SAT scores? Why, why, why, why . . . ?*

As she pushes through the door and into Mrs. Carruthers's tiny cube-shaped office, Jane knows she should feel nervous. But she's just too exhausted.

"Jane!" Mrs. Carruthers says with a blinding smile. She stands up and clasps her hands together. "So? What do you have for me today? Harvard? Yale? Boston Conservatory?"

Jane flops into the cheap wood-and-vinyl chair next to the counselor's desk. She tries to think of a lie. An excuse. But she can't do it. Not right now. She doesn't have the energy anymore.

"I don't have anything," she says.

The guidance counselor's smile falters. There isn't an adult in her life who wouldn't be surprised if Jane told them she just didn't do something she 'd been instructed to do.

"What?" Mrs. Carruthers says, perching on the edge of her chair. "You must have done *something*."

"I'm sorry," Jane says, staring at the cheesy, supposedly uplifting poster above Carruthers's head. There's a guy running in too-short shorts under the word *Determination*.

"Jane?" Mrs. Carruthers says, studying Jane's face with her kind brown eyes. She seems to notice for the first time that Jane is unkempt, unshowered, and unhappy. "Is everything okay with you?" she asks.

No. I don't understand why I'm doing this anymore. Can you tell me why? Why do I have to be perfect?

Jane lifts her heavy eyelids and looks into Mrs. Carruthers's sweet, open, caring face. Suddenly she's struck with a hopeful thought. The first she's had in days. This person is a college *guidance* counselor. She's here to help her—to guide her. Not to judge.

Is it possible? Can she really tell Mrs. Carruthers what's going on?

"If there's anything you need to talk about, Jane, please, feel free," Mrs. Carruthers says. "That's why I'm here."

Jane looks down at her hands. She feels her palms start to sweat as she clasps them together. Can she do it? Can she really tell someone what she's been thinking?

"Okay, here it is," Jane says, still staring at her fingers. "What if I went to a state school?"

She glances at Mrs. Carruthers. Her mouth has dropped open.

"I mean . . . what if I want to go somewhere social? Somewhere with a good football team and a big campus and a—"

"Jane, I'm sorry, I have to interrupt you," Mrs. Carruthers says. "I . . . I don't think you can mean what you're saying."

Jane swallows hard, trying to quell her sudden nausea.

"Um . . . yeah . . . I do mean it," she says.

Mrs. Carruthers looks down at the paperwork on her desk—all of Jane's report cards filled with A's, her awards, letters of recommendation, extracurriculars.

"Jane . . . ," Mrs. Carruthers says finally. "Not only would you be selling yourself short, but you'd be taking a spot from someone else. Someone who would apply to the SUNYs as their reach schools."

"Yeah, but—"

"I can't condone that," Mrs. Carruthers says firmly. "You've worked too hard to throw it all away now, Jane. Now . . . have you spoken to your parents about this. Because I can't imagine that they would approve. Maybe we

174

should call them and set up a meeting so we can all sit down and talk about—"

Jane stands up before the woman can finish her sentence and storms out of the office, suddenly filled with adrenaline. No one cares what she wants. No one cares how she feels. It's all about what her *parents* think is right for her. What her *parents* feel about her future. All she is to anyone is grades . . . success . . . the picture of perfection. And little do they know that she's not even that anymore.

Because you haven't told them. Because you've been lying. Because you're afraid. Why are you still doing this? Why?

By the time Jane hits the hallway, hot tears are streaming down her face. She looks around and everything from the brightly colored bulletin boards to the chipped white water fountain makes her feel trapped. She has to get out of here . . . now. Jane runs for the exit, clueless as to where she's going. All she knows for sure is that she's got to get some air.

"I can't do this anymore," she mutters through her sobs, hugging herself once she gets outside. "I can't."

• • •

Reed stares down at his untouched lunch on Friday afternoon, wondering how anyone could possibly call the muck they serve in the cafeteria food. He's about to get up and ask if anyone wants to go out for lunch when the cafeteria door opens and Karyn walks in. Their eyes lock instantly and Reed is struck with the urge to run. He's been avoiding Karyn for days now—ever since he went all psycho on her in the hall outside the gym. With all these feelings bubbling up about T. J. lately, it's harder than ever to face Karyn, knowing she and his brother are together.

But it's too late. She's seen him and she knows he knows she's seen him. Escape is not an option.

Karyn walks over to the end of the table and looks down at him. "Hey," she says uncertainly.

"Hey," he says back, pulling the brim of his cap lower on his forehead.

"Can we talk?" she asks.

Reed stands up and dumps his tray in the nearest garbage can.

"Come on," he says. Then he stuffs his hands in his pockets and sidles over to the wall, where no one will be able to overhear them.

"So . . . ," she says, leaning back against the wall.

"I'm *really* sorry about . . . the other day," Reed blurts out.

"It's okay," Karyn says automatically.

"No . . . I had no right to blow up at you like that," Reed says. He shakes his head in frustration. "It's just . . . I have a lot going on right now and I took it out on you." He takes a deep breath, getting up the courage to look at her again. "I'm really sorry."

"I understand," Karyn says. Then she turns so that her shoulder is against the wall and smiles up at him. "So . . . Reed Frasier has *stuff* to deal with. Who knew?"

"Believe it or not, my life is not perfect," Reed says, going for levity. But his tone sounds heavy. He blushes and looks away. Karyn is the last person he can lay his problems on. Not when they're problems about his relationship with T. J.

"Hey," she says, tugging at his sleeve.

Reluctantly Reed turns to her again.

"Listen, if you ever want to talk about it . . . whatever it is, I'm here," she says sincerely. "I mean, God knows you've dealt with enough of my melodrama." That look comes back into her eyes—the one he's seen a couple of times recently. Like she's puzzling something together, but it's not fitting. He's about to ask her if she's okay, but then she gives her head a quick shake and the look's gone. "Okay?" she asks him gently.

Reed stares down at the floor so she won't see how affected he is by this conversation. "Yeah, thanks," he says, shoving his hands deeper into his pockets.

For a moment they just stand there in silence, and Reed has never felt so relieved. These last couple of days without Karyn have been hideous. Just standing with her makes him feel better about everything. Everything but the fact that he still wants her and can't have her.

But T. J. isn't here now, Reed thinks.

"So . . . I think it's *your* turn to take *me* out to lunch," he says with a smile. Maybe he'll even be able to get her to spill what's been on her mind.

"Done," Karyn says, grabbing his hand and sending a chill of excitement all the way up his arm. "Let's get out of here."

And for the next half hour, Reed decides to pretend that T. J. doesn't even exist.

• • •

After driving around aimlessly for over an hour, Danny lets himself do what he's been thinking about doing since he left school that afternoon and turns the Jeep toward Cori's house. He stops right next to the curb in front of her house, throws the car into park, and lets his hands fall into his lap.

"What the hell am I doing?" he mutters, tipping his head forward and resting it on the steering wheel.

He wants to apologize for his insane behavior the night before, but he has no idea how to do it. He wants to tell her what's really wrong with him, but he's afraid. He wants to stop feeling guilty and uncomfortable every time he sees her, but if he unloads the truth, he may never see her again.

"So what the hell am I doing?" Danny repeats.

There's a sudden knock at his window and Danny bolts up straight, his pulse racing. Cori is standing right next to him, separated only by the thin layer of glass, and she does not look happy. Shaking, Danny rolls down the window.

"Were you planning on ringing the doorbell or were you just going to set up residence out here?" she asks, hugging her leather jacket closer to her body. She looks beautiful. As always.

"I . . . uh. I need to talk to you," Danny says.

Cori just stares at him for a moment. Then she flips her hair over her shoulder and sighs. "Fine. Unlock the doors."

Danny pops the automatic locks and Cori walks around the car and climbs in. The Jeep is instantly filled with the smell of her shampoo. He loves the way she smells. But the moment she looks at him again, he remembers why he's here and he swallows hard.

You can't have her. It'll never work. Sooner or later it's all just going to blow up in your face, the little voice in Danny's mind chides. *Witness last night. Just do what you came here to do and get out of here.*

"So?" she says, raising her eyebrows. "Talk."

Danny reaches up and grips the steering wheel until his knuckles turn white. The problem is, he no longer knows what he should do. Should he apologize for the scene in the arcade, try to make up, and then risk it happening again? Or should he just be a jerk about it, totally alienate her, and never have to worry about losing it in front of her again?

"You know, I don't know what's going on with you, but if you're not going to apologize for blowing me off, I'm just gonna leave," Cori says, breaking the silence.

She reaches to open the car door and Danny's hand shoots out to grab her other arm. Cori pauses, but she doesn't look at him.

"I'm bipolar," Danny says, squeezing his eyes shut.

"Huh?" Cori says, turning to face him.

"I'm bipolar, manic-depressive, whatever you want to call it," Danny says, releasing her.

Cori sits back in her seat and says nothing. She's just looking at him.

"Sometimes I'm totally depressed for no reason, and sometimes I'm totally happy for no reason, and sometimes I act out like I did with Boyle, and sometimes I'm totally normal." He pauses for breath. She's still staring. "And that's why I got into the accident and it's why I bolted last night and it's why I didn't kiss you the other night because I don't want you to be with me thinking I'm one person and then find out I'm not . . . that . . . person."

Danny stops and his face turns bright red. He can't believe he just said all that out loud. There's a split second of silence, and then Cori's laughter fills the car.

"This isn't funny," Danny says quietly.

"Yeah, it is," Cori says through her laughter.

"You think it's funny that I'm bipolar?" Danny asks.

"No!" she says. "I think it's funny that you think that's a reason I wouldn't want to be with you."

Danny blinks. "Oh," he says, leaning back in his seat and staring out the windshield as he tries to figure out what, exactly, she means by that. Trying to deal with the fact that she's actually laughing. In all the times he's imagined this conversation, laughter never factored in.

"I can't believe you never told me about this. What's the big deal? Everyone I know has *something*." She studies him for a moment, tilting her head. "Personally? I just think it makes you more interesting."

Danny raises his eyebrows. "Seriously?"

"Yeah," Cori says.

"So you don't care," he says, his heart skipping around crazily.

"Please!" Cori says, waving her hand. "Want to know what I *do* care about?"

"What?" Danny asks, still trying to process all of this.

She leans in close to him. So close, he can barely focus his eyes on her nose. "The fact that I haven't heard an apology yet," Cori says with a smile.

A grin spreads slowly across Danny's face. His whole body is charged with intense excitement as he lifts both his arms and rests them on Cori's shoulders. "I'm sorry about last night," he says, his lips mere millimeters from hers.

"Prove it," Cori says.

So Danny kisses her. And it's perfection.

● ● ●

That night, after an endless band practice, Jane arrives home to find both her parents' cars in the driveway. Her shoulders immediately slump even further. The trip to Boston. Somehow she'd forgotten all about it.

She trudges inside and goes directly to her room to pack. Pack for the trip that means nothing. Pack for yet another weekend of playing the perfect Jane.

Why? Why, why, why, why?

Jane has gotten so used to the repeated question in her mind, she barely notices it anymore. She uses her foot to shove open the door and freezes in her tracks. Both her parents are standing by her desk. Her mother lifts her hand from Jane's mouse and her father looks up from one of her drawers, clutching a sheet of paper in each of his hands. From the looks of the pages, they're just old tests, but he's been going through her stuff. Looking for something. Looking, no doubt, for her scores.

They both look guilty. Guilty and angry.

"What are you doing?" Jane asks, dropping her bags on the floor.

I can't do this anymore. I can't—

Her father shoves the papers into the drawer and slams it. Her mother crosses her arms over her chest and glares. Jane feels like she's shrinking down to the size of a pea. She usually only has to deal with one of them at a time. And she's never been ambushed like this, in her own room.

"I called Boston Conservatory today, Jane," her mother says.

Oh God, Jane thinks, her pulse racing through her veins, pounding in her head, seizing up her heart. *It's happening. It's really, really happening. It's all unraveling, right here, right now.*

"I wanted to make sure you had an appointment to meet with someone this weekend, but they told me they didn't have a tape from you."

Jane lowers herself onto her bed, weak. Her brain struggles for an explanation. Any explanation. Anything that will make them keep believing she's their perfect daughter. Their little overachiever. Anything that will keep them from seeing the truth and loathing her for it.

Why, Jane? Why are you still trying?

"I, of course, was indignant," her mother continues, gaining conviction with every word. "I told them that was impossible. That my daughter sent her tape in months ago. That it's always been my daughter's *dream* to go to the conservatory."

At the word *dream* Jane's fear and panic are joined by a twinge of another emotion. A twinge of anger.

Why, Jane. Why?

"So they kindly looked again and guess what they found?" her mother continues. "A FedEx that had arrived *today*." She steps in front of Jane. "I'd like an explanation, Jane."

Jane takes a deep breath, lifts her head, but doesn't even have time to form a sentence.

"What *I'd* like an explanation for is the fact that you skipped Academic Decathlon practice earlier this week," her father says, his breathing labored as if he's been working up to this for hours. "And that you skipped your volunteer responsibilities—"

"You've been checking up on me?" Jane asks, her mouth hanging open in shock.

"Yes, I have, young lady," her father says. "I think I have the right to know that you're throwing your life away. And there's something else I'd like to know. How is it that you are the only student in the district who hasn't received her SAT scores yet?"

"Yes, Jane," her mother puts in. "How gullible do you think we are?"

Snapping her mouth closed and swallowing hard, Jane stares up at their livid faces, searching . . . searching for a response. Searching for the perfect line that will smooth everything over. Appease them. Make them think everything is fine.

But at the same time, Jane feels her anger starting to mount. It crowds out the desperate panic. The desperate need to make them believe she's still their perfect daughter.

How can they do this to her? They've practically been *spying* on her. Calling her teachers and advisers. Going through her stuff? If they're so worried, why haven't they sat her down and asked her to talk?

Why, Jane? Why are you still pretending? Why?

And for the first time, there's an answer. A real, solid answer.

"There's no reason," Jane says aloud, gripping her bedspread at her sides with both hands.

"Excuse me?" her mother spits out, her brow furrowed.

Jane looks up at her parents and her heart is still pounding with fear, but her adrenaline rush is overpowering. She stands up and faces them. Looks them each in the eye.

"Do you even care about me at all?" she asks, her face burning.

"What? Of course we do! Why do you think we're asking you all of this?" her father answers, incredulous.

"You're not here because you care about *me*," Jane says,

her hands clenching into fists, her nails cutting into her palms. "All you care about is my grades, my awards, my meets." With every word the fear dies down a bit more and Jane gains a little more strength. A little more determination to do what she has to do. "That's not caring about *me*. You don't even know how I feel. You never ask how I feel. You never want to know what *I* want. *I* don't matter to you, do I? *I* don't even factor in!"

She's shouting now, and her parents are staring at her, their eyes wide, their mouths forming identical, surprised little o's. If Jane wasn't so upset, she'd think it was funny.

"So you want my scores? You want to see how your little overachiever did? I understand," she says sarcastically. "I mean, you've only been waiting for this moment since the day I was *born!*" Jane turns around, lifts up her mattress, and, ignoring the screaming voice in her head that's begging her not to do it, she shoves the sheet of paper right under her parents' noses. "There! There are my SAT scores. Are you happy now?"

Hands shaking, her mother takes the sheet of paper gingerly out of Jane's grasp. Suddenly both her parents look as though they are going to break into little pieces and crumble all over the floor. But Jane doesn't care. She's never felt so much anger before in her life.

"So? Aren't you going to say anything? Aren't you going to *congratulate* me?" Jane says sarcastically.

Her mother is the first to speak. "Jane . . . what . . . what happened? How could this—?"

"Why didn't you tell us?" her father asks, taking the page and turning it over and over in his hands. "You had to have known, Jane. Why didn't you tell us?"

His big brown eyes are filled with sorrow and disappointment. Jane feels sick just looking at him.

"Because," she says, focusing on the floor. Maybe now they'll realize. Maybe now they'll finally start listening to her. Finally realize that she actually has feelings, thoughts, ideas about her own life. "Because I didn't want you to look at me like that. I didn't want you to know—"

"Well, you'll just have to take them again," her father interrupts, squelching all of Jane's hopes. His voice is firm, stern, determined, even a little bit panicked. "You'll take them in January. There's another test in January, right?" He looks at her mother, desperate.

"Yes, there is. It's not too late, Jane," her mother says, her voice gaining strength. "We can talk to all the deans. We can explain—once you explain to *us*, of course. We can—"

"No!" Jane blurts out, causing both her parents to freeze. She can't believe this is happening. They really *don't* care about her. And she realizes in a rush that maybe that's the reason. Maybe she's been putting this moment off for so long because she didn't want to know for sure what she'd suspected all along.

Her parents really, truly don't care. And suddenly, all she wants to do is hurt them as much as they've hurt her.

"I'm not going to Boston this weekend," she says, her

voice quavering. "I'm not going to an Ivy League school; I'm not going to a conservatory. In fact, after speaking to my guidance counselor this afternoon, I've decided I'm not going anywhere."

"Jane . . . ," her mother says finally. "How could you—"

"No!" Jane screams, surprising even herself. "No more questions! I don't want to hear it anymore! I don't want to hear about how I've let you down or what you want me to be or where you want me to go! I want you out of my room! Both of you! Just get out!"

Stunned into speechlessness, her mother turns on her heel and storms out of the room, quickly followed by her father, who's still clutching her scores. Jane slams the door behind them and locks it, then breaks down into convulsing sobs.

It's over. It's finally, finally over.

She lies down on her bed and just lets herself go, crying and crying and crying until she feels like there's nothing left inside her. *They listened to me,* she thinks, letting the irony seep in. *They left when I told them to leave. They actually listened to me.*

Then, for the first time in days, Jane falls into a deep, deep sleep.